PASSIONS AND PROTECTORS

BEAUTIFUL BEASTS ACADEMY

KIM FAULKS

MILA YOUNG

DEDICATION

A dedication to family and friends who support us, who always stand tall behind us, who keep us going through thick and thin. We love you.

Mila and Kim, a.k.a Kila Foung

Love is savage. Love is fierce. Love will stand beside you when the rest of the world turns their back. Love will claim its weapon of choice....my heart.

There's a murderer on the loose...and mortals are calling for a name to bring to justice.
A name that answers on behalf of the Ancient.
My name...Morwenna Livingstone.
My parents can't reach me.
My best friend doesn't even know where I've gone.
And as mortal deaths continue to plague Tricks City I'm called to stand before the tribunal of mortals and monsters and answer for the crime of conspiracy to murder.
Because I know who the real killer has been all this time.
I just couldn't bring myself to face him.
The betrayal.
The heartache...
And the end.

I DID NOT DO THIS

"I want to call my parents." I lifted my head and met the cold, cruel gaze of a killer.

Silver pupils trapped by midnight irises.

Slayer.

His name conjured a tremor.

I knew who he was...knew that once Slayer had you in his sights, you weren't around for much longer. But the one thing I didn't know was...why he was fixated on me? "I'm entitled to that, right? Or is that only for mortals?"

The two detectives looked to him for a response. But the henchman just straightened on the other side of the stainless steel table and flicked his gaze to the open file in front of me. "Look again."

I shook my head, holding onto his inhuman stare even as my knees trembled. "I've looked...I don't know what you want me to say. I've told you everything...*I did not do this.*"

He leaned forward once more. His long leather trench coat creaking as he braced his hands on the edge. "*Look again.*"

I tried to ready myself, tried not to see the things they

wanted me to see. I tried not to remember the man who made a fool of me in front of a room of the most influential of their kind. I tried not to see a mortal...but it was no use.

Crimson splashes. An arm twisted to a wrong angle. The eyes of a man, wide terror-filled eyes staring back at me. But he wasn't just *any* mortal, was he?

I stared into the lifeless eyes of Commissioner Neil Jordain and swallowed a shudder.

"I think you know more than you're telling us," Slayer murmured. "I think you did this...in fact, *I know*."

There was a sharp knock on the door. Long strands of white hair fell across his eyes as he whipped his gaze to the frosted glass. "I told you no interruptions."

One of the mortal detectives moved, striding toward the door. I couldn't look away...couldn't stop myself from hoping as he yanked open the door. Murmurs came through the crack before it closed once more.

"They're ready." The detective glanced toward the towering immortal and then looked away.

They didn't like him here, that was plain to see.

If they were smart, they'd watch their back. Just like I had to watch mine.

"You and I are going on a little road trip." Slayer turned from the mortal and gripped my gaze.

I clamped my thighs together and shook my head. "I'm not going anywhere, not without calling my father."

Jaw muscles bulged. A nerve twitched at the corner of his eye before Slayer gave a single nod. The same detective opened the door, but this time he let it swing all the way open.

And I looked at my escape.

I'd been here for hours...answering question after question, all while relentless thoughts filled my head. But as heavy steps rang out, I knew hope was coming for me...hope was going to get me out of this place. But the steps heading toward me were too light for my father's and too short for Chuck's.

I held my breath as Nefarious Leathers rounded the doorway and filled the space. "Morwenna." He glanced at Slayer and then quickly away.

There was something in the teacher's gaze, something that shimmered like it was alive.

I shoved from the chair, leaving the bloody images right where they belonged...in front of another person...*because I had nothing to do with this.*

"We have to go with them." Nefarious glanced to the detectives.

"Go with them where?" Panic tore across my chest...my breaths quickened as the two mortals moved, striding toward us.

"We're going on a little road trip." Slayer rounded the edge of the table and grasped my arm. "*And you're coming with me.*"

I cowered from his touch and tried to yank my arm from his hold, but it was useless. He was just like the table I'd left behind; cold, hard, unfeeling and as I looked into Nefarious' eyes I knew there was nothing he could do to stop it.

He just stepped to the side and lowered his gaze as he let the henchman drag me toward the doorway. But I wasn't going anywhere...not without a fight.

"I don't want to go." I thrashed, digging in my heels as I twisted and pulled in his grasp. "Let *me go!* I don't want to do this. Nefarious...*Nefarious! Don't let them take me...*"

"It's okay," he called out behind me. "I'm coming too."

"No."

I jerked my gaze over my shoulder, watching the detective turn on him. "You're not."

"I stand for the Ancient, Vlad Visille." Nefarious rose to his full height. "And as guardian of his Understudy, I command you to let me accompany her."

Terror was closing in, the scent of terror and fear stifling. The squeal of my boots rang out on the hard, concrete floor. *Don't let them take me alone...don't let them...*I lifted my gaze to the eyes of the killer next to me as he spoke. "Let the teacher come."

Relief washed over me as Nefarious shot me a terrified glance and then started walking, pushing in between the two detectives.

I stopped struggling, letting the ache of Slayer's fingers slide over my arm as we left the interrogation room behind. One shove of the double doors and we were in the busy precinct I'd been taken through by Balefire's guards.

Did they know why I was here?

Did Balefire send them?

I tried to search for answers to any of this—just as I had when they bought me in here.

I found nothing but lonely silence and an ache in my chest.

Mortals turned their head to look at me as Slayer dragged me out of the narrow hallway and into the waiting room.

"Hey, *bloodsucker!*" A man called and stumbled toward me slurring his words and swaying his hand as he headed toward me. "I *fucking hate you.*"

I swallowed his pain and rage and looked away.

"*Kill them!*" he screamed. "*Kill them all!*"

Slayer never flinched, in fact he didn't even notice the outburst. This Vampire took heartless to a whole new level.

He didn't care about me...or his own kind. That was easy to see. All he cared about was parading me through the packed waiting area like a criminal.

They all looked at me, some sneered, some widened their eyes.

Men, women...

Mortals.

Until we strode through the automatic doors at the front of the precinct and out into the night. The sky was brightening in the distance. Morning was sneaking in through the edge of the horizon. I'd been here for hours...and it seemed there was no end to the madness in sight.

Two silver, unmarked cars were parked out front of the towering station. One of the detectives rushed forward, hitting the button on the remote. Orange lights flared in the darkness as Slayer strode toward the rear door.

He yanked the handle, swinging the door open wide. "Get in."

I glanced to Nefarious, watching him look to the henchman.

"I won't tell you again." The threat was clear, *do it, or he'll make me.*

My legs trembled as I stepped off the footpath and climbed inside. The bitter stench of cigarettes and death bloomed as I lowered myself down to the seat. The door closed beside me with a *thud.*

"Let me in there," Nefarious demanded.

But there was no demanding the Slayer, not if you wanted to stay *undead.* A deep snarl came from the killer as he strode past Mr. Leathers and rounded the rear of the car, heading to the other side.

My teacher strode after him, hot on his tail. "I'm not letting you take her, not without me. You might kill me, but you know the repercussions of that. The Council will be hearing about this...oh yes, it will."

Slayer did the one thing I didn't expect, he slowed his steps on the other side of the car and then turned to Nefarious. "Say one more word to me and I'll tear open your throat and drink the pathetic blood from your body."

My hand was already rising, fingers clawing the inside of the door, searching for a way out as the rear door opened on the other side and Nefarious climbed in. Dark eyes glinted as they met mine. He glanced to my hand on the door, and gave the tiniest shake of his head.

There was fear in his eyes, real, terrifying fear as he slid across the seat until he was beside me. Slayer pushed in too, cramming me against the door as the detective slid in behind the wheel.

The engine started with a growl. It was barely a second before we were rolling, pulling out onto the street to merge with the sparse morning traffic.

"Where are we going?" I murmured and then glanced to Nefarious.

"I wish I knew," he answered but kept his gaze straight ahead.

Bright lights washed over us from the car behind. I followed Nefarious' lead, taking note of the street signs as we worked our way through Tricks City. Darkened shops gave way to clusters of houses as we entered the suburbs.

I knew where we were going the minute I caught the glittering lights up on the hill. Trickery Hill some people called it, but others called it by another name; the Power of Tricks City.

Anyone who was anyone lived on that hill. Senators, Army Generals, District Attorneys. My stomach clenched in warning. "I know where we're going."

I turned my head to silver eyes glinting in the dark. He was watching me from across the seat, taking in my every reaction, and my every move. The moment the car started to climb, I grew terrified. I turned, clawed the side of the door once more. "Let me out of here...*I said, let me out!*"

But there was no handle, not even a button to wind down the window. There was nothing but smooth leather over hardened steel. I jerked my gaze to the detective. "Let me out of this car right now...or..."

"Or what, Morwenna?" Slayer answered. "Or you'll do what?"

Hurt them?

Tear apart this car?

Go on a rampage and kill a man I barely know...just like the Commissioner?

I gulped the air as the bright sparks of the hill came closer, only they weren't glittering like diamonds. They were rubies and sapphires. Red and blue...*red and blue,* splashing in my eyes as we crested the rise.

There were cars everywhere crammed on the side of the road...and people too. They turned as we drove toward them, some still clothed in pajamas and sweatpants. I took in the neighbors, the police, everyone staring with confusion as we approached the oversized mansion. My stomach ached. I didn't want to be here.

I couldn't do this, and panic clawed at my chest. I gripped the door, desperate to escape and run.

The front gates lay open like a gaping mouth, and we pulled into the driveway. Cop vehicles and unmarked cars crowded the front of the three story home.

I shifted in my seat, unable to sit still, unable to stop thinking about Slayer's words, unable to believe they were implicating me.

We stopped outside a towering sandstone house with its manicured lawns and massive bubbling fountain in the front yard. Slayer climbed out before shoving the door shut with a thump.

I couldn't move. My gaze gripped by the open front door as men in plastic overalls walked through.

Nefarious glanced my way. "I'll be with you."

"I didn't do this." The words fell from my mouth, and when I tilted my head back, meeting his gaze, I saw the fear slithering behind his dark gaze. I swallowed hard. "What am I meant to do?"

"Whatever Slayer asks you. Tell him the truth. He can smell a lie better than any immortal alive."

My door opened with a creak and he stood here, tall and ominous like Death come to collect his latest victim.

"Come on, let's get this over with. The sooner they figure out they have the wrong Vampire, the sooner we can all get back to our lives." Nefarious shook his head, climbing out the other side.

I willed myself to move and climbed outside. A cold wind pushed against me, attempting to reverse my steps back into the car.

Officers stood outside the grand home that must have once brought this family joy.

Slayer growled for me to follow him, and with my head low, I tracked his footsteps into the house, Nefarious close on my heels.

"*Murderer!*" a female shrieked, echoing through the enormous house.

Footfalls raced toward me, the click clack of heels like thunder. I lifted my head as she tore through down the hallway and headed my way. Silver hair whipped the air and her black dress billowed as she ran. Her pale skin streaked with lines of black mascara. *A ruined date...that's what it looked like...a ruined date.*

"You killed him," she screamed, nails slashing the air as she hurtled toward me. "You killed my Neil. You *filthy bloodsucking monster!*"

One of the detectives was there, stepping in front of her, and wrapping her arms around her carefully. "It's okay, Diane. It's okay."

"I didn't do this," the hollow words slipped from my lips.

She fought against the detective, her eyes glistening with sharp terror of pain. "You *killed him...I fucking know you did!*"

Nefarious pushed me behind him, while two more officers swept in around her. Low muffled voices mingled together in a chorus of...*it's okay, Diane. We're here now, we'll find the evidence...it's okay, we'll find the evidence.*

Inhuman howls of agony turned to mewling whimpers. Heartbroken...soul torn. I tried to swallow, tried to understand how I was here...staring at her. "There's been a mistake," I answered, my words too pathetic for her ears.

She shook her head, her body shuddering as they closed in around her, and gently led her away.

Eyes. I felt everyone's on me, judging me, assuming I was this monstrosity. But if they knew me, they'd know I couldn't be capable of such an act. They'd made a horrible mistake.

Fear crept over me like a chill and locked tight in my gut.

Slayer was on the move again, and I took steps over the tiled entrance hallway, up the curved stairs, and across the lush cream carpet in the bedroom.

Lifting my gaze seemed an impossibility.

"How did you enter his bedroom?" Slayer asked, his voice barren of emotions.

I lifted my head to the four poster bed covered in white silk sheets. Blood stained them, splashing the fabric like rips across flesh.

Sickness rose through me when my attention fell to the splattered blood outline on the carpet.

Commissioner Neil Jordain.

He'd died here and the shadow of his death would forever be etched into this room.

"Did you break into the home through the rear?" Slayer continued.

But the room tilted around me, and I couldn't concentrate. My breakfast rushed to my throat. I clasped my stomach and ran toward the open bathroom door across the bedroom.

Bile hit my throat and I gagged. Skidding to a stop in front of the toilet, I bent over and hurled out everything in my stomach.

Stars danced in my vision as my chest convulsed.

Nefarious stood by my side, pulling my hair off my face, holding it over my shoulders until I finished vomiting. I stumbled over to the sink and flipped on the water before washing out my mouth and splashing my face.

He handed me a towel, and I scrubbed my face before staring in the mirror at my red eyes, horror scribbled all over my expression. I was caught in a nightmare... It felt like I was frozen in place, unsure I could move.

"Mor." Nefarious touched my arm and turned me to face him. "They're waiting for you. Remember, give them no reason to doubt you."

"But I didn't do any of this," I whispered.

"We need to show them." Unspoken words lingered behind his voice. What did he know?

When Slayer stepped into the bathroom, I lost the chance to ask.

I dropped the towel on the sink and nodded. Nefarious was right. I'd done nothing wrong and had to show them. I mean, I didn't even know where the commissioner lived before today.

Back in the bedroom, I stood tall and took in the room with fresh eyes to make sense of the murder and help prove my innocence.

Two of the officers whispered loud enough for me to hear. "Not much of a Vampire."

I cringed but refused to become a victim. I'd done nothing wrong.

Slayer glared my way, trying to decipher what my little stunt in the bathroom was about. I turned my attention to the blood splash, how it looked diagonal on the side of the bedspread, how it was thicker on one side and petered out the farther it traveled. No gun then... a knife was used to slash his body.

"Is there anything you want to tell us?" Slayer's voice shattered the silence, and I flinched. I hated showing him how he affected him.

"W-why do you think I did this?"

Nefarious' words came to mind, but I needed to know how this murder pointed to me.

The corner of Slayer's upper lip curled like he might swear, but instead he ran his tongue over his teeth under his lips. "Answer my question."

"I didn't do this," I blurted. "I've never been to the Commissioner's home or had anything to do with him. This is a mistake."

Slayer stepped toward me in three long strides, and I fought my initial reaction to step back.

"No mistakes," he growled. "Your act back in the bathroom doesn't fool anyone. Now start again and tell me how you did this." He pointed to the white stained carpet, and my sickness returned. When I met Nefarious' gaze, he gave me a slight nod, and I grasped onto that hope that he was on my side.

An hour of Slayer hounding me with the same questions, he finally decided he wasn't going to get any information from me since I had none to give.

"Let's go," he growled and reached out to shove me from the room when Nefarious stepped to my side, blocking his touch.

No words exchanged, I rushed downstairs, glad to be out of there, but I caught a glance of the Commissioner's wife in the lounge room, crying into her hands, and my eyes pricked for her agony and loss.

I moved faster, running out of the house, needing distance from this home.

We climbed into the back of the car, and the detective driver roared the engine to life. "Back to the station. I want a taped confession. I *want* to understand why you did this, and who else was involved."

Desperation surged to the surface. I jerked my gaze to Nefarious as the words spilled free. "No one was involved. They have the wrong person. They have the wrong Vampire."

Why would someone do this?

Why would someone think it was me?

CHAPTER TWO

INTERROGATION

My heart lunged at the sight of the sleek black limousine outside the precinct. I didn't have to look at the number plates to who know who it was. *Dad. Dad is here...he'll know what to do. He'll get me out of this nightmare.*

Nefarious glanced to the limo and then to me. He knew who it was, and the kind of power my father controlled. In the Vampire world there were those who sided with the Ancient powers, and those with the growing stronghold of the Supernatural Council.

But there weren't many, who straddled both sides...*only one.*

Dante Livingstone.

I watched Slayer for a reaction, but he never took his eyes from the road ahead as the unmarked car took a sharp turn and instead of parking outside where Dad waited...they turned into a driveway and then nosed down to the car park underneath.

"What are you doing?" I turned to the street as the

limousine slipped behind the concrete barrier. "What the Hell are you doing?"

The detective glanced into the rear view mirror, but it wasn't me he was looking at. It was Slayer...always fucking Slayer.

"I demand you take me to my father." My hands shook as I shifted in my seat. *"I demand—"*

"You *demand?*" The henchman turned his head, savage eyes blazing with fury. "Murderers don't demand anything."

"She's not been convicted of any crime," Nefarious broke in, slowly turning toward the unmerciful Vampire beside him. "This is a questioning, isn't that correct?"

Chilling, savage silence filled the car.

"I don't see the Ancient waiting for us, or the Council for that matter. If they're not here that only means one thing. This is a fishing expedition, *and nothing more.*"

My mouth went dry, a pathetic *thud* echoed through my chest. No Ancient and no Council meant they weren't serious. Still, that seed of doubt bloomed as the unmarked police car pulled up outside a bank of elevators on the lower ground.

"Why do you think I'm here?" Slayer cut the teacher a glare. "*I* speak on behalf of the Council. When *I* question you for a mortal's murder...you can be confident I have my reasons, and right now...my reason is *her.*" Silver eyes glinted like the steel of a blade.

I could feel the edge of that blade bearing down on the back of my neck. Goosebumps raced across my arms. I'd never felt so vulnerable before...never so *mortal.*

The detective switched off the engine as the second car pulled in behind us and killed their lights. Darkness moved in, even though the underground carpark lights still blazed through the windows.

Reality was a remorseless killer as hope died away. The car door opened beside me, the officer waited. It didn't matter if the limousine was parked outside the precinct...Dad may as well be a million miles away.

He couldn't help me...*no one could.*

"Out," the officer barked at me.

I did what he said, the fight now turning to those I loved. Slayer and Nefarious stepped out of the car behind me as the second detective strode toward the bank of elevators and stabbed the button.

They think it's me.

They think I've done this.

Confusion clouded my own mind as the *ding* of the elevator sounded. Stainless doors opened wide ready to swallow us, and that's exactly how I felt—*swallowed.* Consumed by my answer, drowning in my confusion. I stepped through the doors and moved to the back of the lift. Slayer and Nefarious were in next. I felt the henchman's watchful eyes slowly picking me apart like a vulture, just waiting for me to lay down and die.

We were moving before I realized, rising slowly, one floor at a time. I craned my head as we came to a shuddering stop and the doors opened again. But they weren't parading me through the waiting room like a leper, not anymore. This time it was all hidden, all secret...only because they knew who was waiting for me out there.

My legs trembled as they all moved, striding out, before Slayer turned his head, watching me...*waiting for me.* A numbness washed over me as I moved, following them through a new set of doors to lead us into the same hallway I was in earlier.

The interrogation room was still empty, still alight, the chairs still empty, waiting. It felt like a month since I'd been here...a month of standing inside that house with the heady stench of blood still lingering in the air. But as I stepped inside, I saw something that hadn't been in the office before.

It was a whiteboard covered in pictures. *Pictures of me.* I don't remember moving, don't remember sitting. All I remember were the images of Ava, and the Wolves...*and me.*

"You understand now, right?" Slayer was beside me, breathing fetid heat against my cheek as he leaned over. "You've been behind the murders, the same way as you've been behind everything else. It started with a feud between the Livingstones and the Qurants, didn't it?"

I stared at the images.

"Are you just going to sit there?" the Detective snapped. "Say *something!*"

I didn't do this...I didn't do this...I didn't do this...

"Hermond Qurant, you remember him, *don't you?*" Slayer growled in my ear. "His daughter attended Bestias Academy...until you killed her."

"She attacked me," the words slipped from my lips before I knew. Her dad was Lord Vampire who wanted my dad dead.

Nefarious groaned and snarled. "Don't say *anything,* Morwenna."

But Slayer was shifting his body to block the view of my teacher, and like a shark with the scent of blood he moved in for the kill. "So, you admit you killed her? And her father, someone highly regarded by both the Ancient and the Council."

"He was going to kill us, going to kill my entire family"

"So, you admit it, correct?" Slayer leaned closer, his gaze boring into mine. "And the next image...you were spotted outside a storm drain in the Witches part of the city, a drain that connected to a network of tunnels. We had someone follow your scent, that just so happened to leave us to another dead body."

The darkened image on the whiteboard was a crime scene photo, tiny black markers were numbered one through eight. There was a drop of black Demon blood, a fragment of something that looked like cloth.

"And you still weren't done, were you?" Slayer straightened and walked around the table to the board filled with images. "You decided to slay a room filled with your own classmates."

"That wasn't me." I shook my head. "That was Thorin."

"Thorin, your boyfriend, isn't that correct?"

I flinched at the word *boyfriend* and lifted my gaze to the Vampire. "Ex-boyfriend."

"So you say," he pushed back and turned to the images once more. "A lot of people seem to turn up dead around you Ms. Livingstone. Small intricacies that led you to publicly humiliate the Commissioner Neil Jordain."

"Publicly humiliate?" I muttered. "I was there trying to calm the mortals down. I was doing my job as an Understudy."

He turned to me, his top lip curling. "Is that so?"

"I didn't mean to offend him. And the last time I looked, offending someone isn't a crime."

He reached out, grasped a folder from the detective and threw it onto the table in front of me. "No, you're right, but running someone through with a sword is."

My hand was already rising from my lap, catching the corner of the folder and exposing the lies. It was a picture of me, grainy and black and white...but clear enough. I was walking with a sword. The same sword I'd carried down to the hidden room under the church floor. I glanced down, and the same clothes. "That's not right."

"That is you, *correct?*"

I stared at the image. There was no denying it was me. "It is, but that's not right."

He leaned over the end of the table and snatched the images from my hand. "These were captured by CCTV cameras outside the Commissioner's house at one am this morning, around the time the coroner estimated time of death. So you've been linked to a number of deaths and caught on cameras wearing the same clothes you're in now." He lowered his gaze to my uniform. "And if I'm not mistaken, that's blood right there."

He pointed to a smear and a splatter on the bottom of my shirt. I couldn't breathe, couldn't think...couldn't do anything as the door opened and in came a female uniformed police officer. "Sergeant Lucas is going to escort you into a room. She'll give you a set of clothes to change into while we take these ones."

I jerked my gaze to Slayer and then to Nefarious, and froze. A flicker of doubt crossed his gaze, and the sight of that hit me like a slap.

"Ms. Livingstone," Slayer growled.

I broke Nefarious stare and slowly pushed to my feet. "Will I get them back?"

"No, you won't."

They waited, staring...judge, jury and executioner. I followed the female officer out of the room and down the hall, and all the while she said nothing. This was all a terrible misunderstanding. They'd gotten the wrong CCTV, there was no way a feed like that could be crossed. I thought of the monitoring room back at the Academy. Balefire watched every camera, and scanned every recording.

He had to know that these mistakes don't happen…not like this.

"In there." The officer shoved a door to the bathroom onwards and waited for me to step through.

Bright lights buzzed and flickered overhead. They could take my clothes, they could test the blood all they wanted. It wasn't the commissioner's blood…it wasn't even human.

But is it? That tiny voice inside me whispered as the door behind us swung closed.

"There's a set of clothes there on the counter."

I nodded at the words behind me and glanced to the white shirt and draw-string pants, and in an instant my world started to tremble.

What if I was wrong? What if what they were saying was true? And that I was stupid pawn in someone else's game? Panicked thoughts hit me wave after wave. I started to see things differently, started to piece the events of the last few months together just as they had on that white board.

"Hurry it up, I don't have all day," the officer snarled beside me.

I stepped forward, grasped the stack of clothes and then headed for the stall.

"No, out here, where I can see you."

I froze, clutched the clothes tighter against my body and turned. One glance at the door behind her and I shook my head. "No, someone could see me."

Her hand dropped to her hip, to where the taser sat. Twelve hundred volts for a human, a jolt with that and it's just a sting. But the one on her hip was special, the handle not colored black, but red. Five thousand volts of electricity through poisoned darts would make me hurt for days.

I was already hurting, more than I had in years. I tore

my gaze from her hand, meeting her eyes. She swallowed hard, fear bright and sparkling in her pupils. I lowered my hands, feeling the entire world crushing me and slowly nodded.

I watched her, kicked the back of one boot and yanked my foot free, then the other. My fingers were trembling as I reached for the clasp and the zipper of my skirt. I yanked it down, and stepped out of the skirt and the officer stepped forward holding open a plastic bag. "Panties too."

I flinched, heat rushing to my cheeks. "Why?"

"Panties," she commanded and I lowered my hands to the edge of my hips and slid them down.

Humiliation burned as I dumped my underwear into the bag and hurried to slip on the pants. My shirt was next, and still she held open the bag and glanced to my bra. "No, no way. There's not a speck of anything on there."

Silence and the rattle of plastic was all the answer I received. I reached around, unclasped the hooks and turned my back to her, slipping on the shirt and leaving my bra on the bench as I crossed my arms over my body.

"In the bag," she commanded.

Tears shimmered, making the glaring lights overhead blur. I grasped the bra, shoved my feet into my boots as she shook her head, and reached into her pocket, pulling another bag free.

"You've got to be kidding?"

But she wasn't, and so this nightmare continued, until I picked up my boots and dropped them into the bag. She turned then, grasped the bags in one hand and yanked open the door. I hugged myself, covering my body as she led me back to the interrogation room and waited outside.

Slayer glanced at the bags in her hands as the two detectives strode through the door. I looked to Nefarious, searching his eyes for some hint of what was happening next.

"It's time you returned her to the Academy." Nefarious glanced to Slayer when he spoke, for the henchman was the driving force behind this lunacy.

The hunter glanced toward the detectives and gave a nod. "I'll be watching Ms. Livingstone. You can be guaranteed of that."

With those chilling words ringing in my ears Nefarious strode forward, grasped my elbow and gently pushed me from the room.

"Keep walking," he murmured, propelling me forward with each step. "Don't look back."

My socks made no sound on the concrete floor. I gripped my body tighter, mashing my breasts under my palms as one of the detectives strode ahead, pushing through the door at the end of the hall.

In a second we were through, leaving the horror of that whiteboard and the images behind. Nefarious never gave me a second to falter, driving me through the door at the end of the hall.

"I'm giving you five more goddamn seconds to take me to *my daughter*, or *I'll tear this place apart brick by brick!*" Dad's roar rang through the doorway as I stumbled into the waiting room once.

He leaned over the desk, stabbing his finger at the sergeant, his face a mask of feral rage.

"Daddy!" I stumbled forward.

Dark eyes swung toward me, he scanned my body, and then the clothes I was wearing, before relief swept across his face. "Dear Lucifer," he muttered and strode toward me, holding out his arms.

I'd never felt so small as I did in that moment, never so

weak, never so dependent on another in my entire life. The tears came hard as fast as he wrapped strong arms around me and pulled me against his chest. "It's okay, you're safe now."

One arm dropped from around my back. I pressed myself harder against him, until the sweep of a jacket settled over my shoulders. "Let's get you out of here, okay? Take you home...and then *I'll* deal with this fucking mess."

"No, Sir," the detective answered behind me. "You won't be taking her anywhere."

I lifted my gaze as a nerve twitched near Dad's eye. "Are you telling me how to take care of my own daughter, *detective?*"

Careful, controlled words meant only one thing. Dad wasn't playing...no, he wasn't playing at all. Footsteps rang out and then stilled behind me. I caught Dad shift his gaze to the person behind me. There was a flinch in his eyes, a terrifying understanding.

"As I said to her," the detective drove the point home. "She'll be returning to the Academy...."

Dad lowered his gaze, imploring eyes meeting mine. "You're going to be okay, you hear me?" His hands trembled, pulling me close. "*Stay safe,*" whispered words barely audible against my ear. "*However you can, my sweetheart, until I can fix this.*"

"Let's go." Cruel fingers ground into the muscle of my arm as the detective yanked, tearing me from Dad's arms.

Tears slipped down my cheeks. "Daddy..."

"I promise you, Morwenna." Agony filled his face as he took a step toward me. "*I promise you.*"

Shudders ripped across my chest as the detective pulled me once more. Nefarious strode forward, meeting my dad's gaze. I'd never seen Dad so savage...never seen him so *undone.* "I will find out who did this." It wasn't just a warning...*it was a promise.* Nefarious lowered his gaze, out of respect, or just plain fear, before Dad's gaze gravitated to the Vampire behind us. Hate rolled through his eyes as I stumbled toward the front doors and out into the bright glare of the morning.

The worst night of my life was finally over.

CHAPTER THREE

GOODBYES SUCK

"We'll find a way," Nefarious murmured, his eyes dark and lost.

I couldn't stop trembling, every inch of me wanted to run away from everything, but instead, I remained still in Slayer's car. I'd follow his instructions, play by the rules to prove my innocence and pray to hell they didn't find me guilty of crimes I didn't carry out.

Suddenly all I saw were photographs of me pinned to the precinct board. Slayer had followed me and gained every piece of information he could to frame me.

My hand instinctively jerked to the door, desperation choking me. I had to get out, but my door remained locked from the outside.

When I glanced at Nefarious, his deflated posture was the opposite of his encouraging words.

I scanned the Academy grounds as we drove through the front gates, part of me hoping to find Dad's limousine, but he wasn't there, and I sighed heavily.

We pulled up in front of the main building, and with the motor still running, Slayer twisted his head to look at me over his shoulder. "I'll be in touch. Don't plan on leaving the country."

Was that meant to be a joke?

Nefarious shoved open his door and climbed out before shutting me inside alone with the henchman.

"You'll slip up soon enough." Slayer glared at me before he straightened.

Mr. Leathers opened my door and held out his hand, which I accepted, gripping it like a lifeline as I climbed out.

Slayer drove off, the back door shutting of its own accord from the momentum of his speed.

"What am I supposed to do?" I asked, the ache in my stomach deepening.

"We wait, and you do nothing but go to class and back to your dorm. Don't interact with anyone if possible. He's watching your every move."

His words were like daggers in my back. I *was* being watched, and it left me feeling dirty, like someone had ransacked my personal items while I had my back turned, taking what they wanted.

"Got it, keep my nose clean." I tried to smile, to be Mor, the Vamp at the Academy who always found a way out of any sticky mess, but I was fooling myself.

"This isn't a joke," he muttered, his hand reaching for my arm, fingers grazing the white fabric of my shirt. Clothes I'd been given by Slayer to wear while he tested mine.

In my mind I screamed, and my hands curled into balls with fury. What exactly would Slayer find, or was he setting me up to uncover another clue to prove my guilt?

Nefarious' grip tightened.

"I know it's not a joke," I barked and pulled free from his grasp. "I'm so scared, I can barely think straight.

His expression softened and I caught his fear, slithering

behind his gaze. He was scared for me, and I didn't need this. I had enough dread inside me for both of us.

"I've got to go. Thanks for joining me today." I turned away and marched around the building and across the lawn, barely keeping my tears at bay and my knees from knocking together.

The sun fell behind a cluster of clouds, drowning the Academy in shadows, turning the normally lush grounds almost gray. It matched my insides. Broken. Lost. Stressed.

Up ahead, Ava emerged from our dorm with Chuck, Nero, and Judas. I pushed into a faster walk, my mouth pulling into a smile because I needed them. Always did.

But Slayer's words slashed through my mind like a sword, tearing down my confidence and flooding me with doubts. Reminding me of the consequences.

You'll slip up soon enough.

I should have been ecstatic to see my friends and boyfriends again, but dread locked my legs, and I froze in place, concealed by a nearby oak tree.

If Slayer turned his attention on them, then what? He'd accuse them of murder too?

They were my gang, my go to group, and together we solved everything, but this... this was different. If they got a whiff, they'd investigate and draw Slayer's attention.

Panic grew stronger in my chest, reminding me of what was at stake, so I'd tell them something else. Something to do with the Understudy, that I had a new assignment, and I would spend more time with the Ancient and away from class. They'd ask questions... lots of them, but this was the only way. As much as I wanted to run, I couldn't.

Scrubbing a hand down my face, I tried to smile, but it felt wrong and uncomfortable on my mouth.

Shoulders back, I hurried toward my friends, memorizing every small thing about them so I'd never forget them. The way Ava always touched Chuck, a hand, a brush of her elbow; she adored him. My Wolves always stuck together, and they had each other. When it was just the three of them, they rough played, shoving each other about, laughed and barked jokes.

They were mine.

I had all of them, and my lies were about to cut me to pieces.

Ava's head swung in my direction first, and she waved, her mouth curling into a wide grin.

"Hey, where have you been? And why are you dressed like a cult leader?" she murmured.

Right, the white shirt and pants Slayer made me wear. I looked up to Ava and Chuck who waited for an explanation, while my two Wolves closed in toward me, their hands on my arms and back, kisses on my cheek and mouth, and I stood there with the world tilting around me, my explanations vanishing. I couldn't remember them, not when those I cared for the most showed me affection and I planned to lie to them. To keep a secret that might tear them apart if they ever found out.

The swell of panic built inside me like an unstoppable avalanche, while my brain fired out negative thoughts, and sweat dripped down my back.

"This old thing," I huffed, sounding so fake in my mind, and Ava's brow arched because she didn't believe it either.

"It's Nefarious," I blurted the first thing that came to mind.

"Mr. Leathers made you dress like the KKK?" Nero added.

"No," I snapped and lowered my raised shoulders. "It's

part of my Ancient studies. I have to perform some duties off site. Real boring stuff."

Judas' hand cupped the side of my face and turned me to face him. He stared at me with such depth and concern, tears pricked my eyes.

He saw through me, saw my despair and lies, and he'd pick apart my poorly formed web of lies.

"What's going on, Mor? Talk to me."

"Is everything okay?" Chuck asked.

Desperate words shoved to the front of my mind, eager to tumble out, and despite my better judgement, those thoughts dangled in front of me.

But they were selfish reasons.

Reasons to ensure I didn't face this alone.

Then, they'd be pulled in front of the firing squad with me. This was where I stepped up and protected those I loved. With my life if it came down to it.

I knew what I had to do.

I had to bear the consequences on my own.

So, with every inch of inner strength, I leaned into Judas' touch and closed my eyes, inhaling his timbery fresh scent, tucking it into my mind. When I looked at him again, I was a new person, one who wore a mask, and offered him a genuine smile.

"Everything is perfect. I just need to miss a few classes for this Understudy gig, but I'll catch up on assignments. So, I won't be around for a week or so. Might be quicker. Anyway, I need to change out of these gross clothes."

"Wait! You're gonna be gone for a couple of weeks? Where will you stay?" Ava reached for my hand, taking it in hers. "I don't like this."

"It won't be long, promise. Not sure where I'm staying yet as it's all top secret."

Her expression fell and my worry slid back into place; it killed me to push them away.

I dragged her into my arms. "Trust me. With you in Chuck's arms, you won't notice I'm gone. I'll be back soon enough." My lies were knives slicing my dead heart.

But I had to put distance between me and them.

"We better go," Ava said. "We've got P.E. class next so put on your sexy little shorts, babe." She broke away, her voice distant, and I nodded at Chuck with a confirmation everything was fine and dandy.

His gaze hardened on me, his hands fisted like he might explode into a rant and force me to spill the truth. He knew me better than most, and I stiffened, expecting him to challenge me. He didn't normally sit back and do nothing... that wasn't him. Yet, he seemed to shake as if fighting with himself.

Judas' breath hitched. "Shorts, you say?" His voice broke the uncomfortable stillness.

I laughed, falling into his arms, and let him kiss me, refusing to look at Chuck. I welcomed Nero, who joined us. But on the inside, I was breaking.

"You had us worried," Judas murmured. "Don't ever vanish like that again."

My response wouldn't come at first, not when my throat choked up.

As they started toward class, I held my ground and my hand slipped out of their hands. They glanced back at me, all of them. "I can't go with you."

Tears pinched the corners of my eyes.

"You're starting the extra studies now?" Judas snapped.

I nodded and already their hurt expressions blurred behind my gaze. Chuck's face hardened further, his jawline clenching, yet he still said nothing.

"I'll be in touch. Love you all." I turned away as tears rolled down my face, as my chest felt like it cracked in half, and no matter how much my legs trembled and my heart ripped to shreds, I didn't look back at them. I wasn't strong enough to face them. And I wanted distance between Chuck and me, fast.

I was doing this to protect them, to keep them safe. Maybe one day they'd forgive me and understand.

With rapid steps, I hurried into my building and raced into my room. I shut the door and let it take my weight as I slid my ass to the ground and cried. The sobs punched through me, tearing my body, my bones, my guts. The pain came in waves, brief moments of calmness appeared, only to be ripped back into the arms of grief. I cried for everything I was close to losing: my friends, my lovers, my parents, and...my life.

Unsure how much time passed, I wiped away the tears and climbed to my feet. I dragged myself into the closet and pulled out a backpack then tossed it on the bed, along with a few changes of clothing and anything else I might need.

My hands wouldn't stop shaking and the tears kept flowing. I was so fucking scared, unsure what came next, what I was supposed to do. But I also knew if I was under investigation, my friends and family would be soon too. I couldn't bring them into his mess... I wouldn't. I had to go some place no one would look for me, including the henchman, and then I'd figured everything the fuck out.

I hurled clothes into my bag, not really looking at what I'd grabbed, and added a pair of shoes and toiletries. I zipped it all up and started stripping, pulling the top up and over my head, then pushing down my pants. Ava called them cult clothing, but they resembled a prison outfit to me.

Grabbing a pair of jeans and black hoodie, I got dressed

and stepped into black sneakers. Everything was about comfort and being practical right now. My phone beeped with a message from Ava.

Love and miss you already, followed by a heart emoji.

I wiped fresh tears from my eyes and sent back a quick pulsing heart GIF, but before shutting my phone, I caught Dad's number in my address list. Swallowing hard, my fingers twitched with the need to call him, message him, anything. But if Slayer watched me, then he'd sure as hell be tracking my phone messages too, maybe even tapped into my calls. Even bugged my room.

Dad had been through enough lately with the curse and everything. Plus, he'd find out everything from the precinct and maybe even Slayer, but like everyone else in my life, I had to keep my distance for now.

With my bag in hand, I headed to the door, ready to leave. One look back at my room and I made myself a promise. I'd find a way to return to the Academy and all my friends. Whatever it took.

CHAPTER FOUR

FAMILIAR SURROUNDINGS

The Academy grounds lay quiet. Students and teachers sat in class while I crossed the lush lawn with hurried steps, my bag swinging over a shoulder. I'd stay low for a few days or however long it took and work out my next steps.

Nerves danced over my flesh, and I kept checking over my shoulder, expecting someone to call my name.

My throat was parched, and everything swam around me in a blurred mess. I held my chin high and kept going, needing time to work everything out. To protect those I adored. And to keep some distance from Slayer for as long as possible.

Up ahead, the church came into view. The building was worn with time, and it always conjured dark memories for me, from being paralyzed by a hex from Brylee, encountering Brutus, and even us discovering the Academy's dark, dirty secrets. Maybe this was my turn to add my own footprint on this ancient relic.

The front steps creaked under my feet, and I shoved open the front door before shutting it behind me.

Heavy cobwebs hung from the corners, and layers of dust coated every surface. Shattered windows, holes in the walls and ceiling screamed of abandonment. No one came here, unless it was for a prank or something more sinister, so this place would be perfect to hide in.

I glanced at the latch in the middle of the church floor and hurried closer. I bent down and grabbed the large metal ring before wrenching it up, the wood groaning as it gaped open.

Darkness peered back, and a familiar fear closed in around me because unlike last time, when we'd encountered Brutus, I was alone.

Crouching low, I reached down to find the ladder. One step lower, then another, I climbed down and pulled the trap door closed behind me, throwing me into darkness. I'd been here before, and with the heaviness of the world on my shoulders, I'd rather confront a spirit than Slayer.

I toed the landing and quickly jumped down. I unzipped my bag before stuffing my hand inside and rummaged until my fingers touched the smooth surface of a candle and lighter. In haste, I lit the wick, illuminating the room, giving it life. Cabinets and old desks filled the place, along with a small dusty couch in the corner, which would be perfect with a bit of cleaning.

From my bag, I pulled out another thick candle and set them both on the nearest desk. Then I retreated and flopped onto the couch, a plume of dusk billowing up. But I didn't care. I drew my knees to my chest, hugging my legs.

Despite the dimness and the musty smell, relief fell over me. I'd found a place to hide until I came up with a plan to deal with Slayer and the accusations against me. But I felt lost and miserable, the sensation sinking through every cell of my body.

Nothing but the faint crackle of candlelight sounded, and I studied the peeling green wallpaper that had long ago blistered and faded. Everything in this building was falling apart, just like me... exhausted and broken.

I couldn't remember how long I sat in the shadows, how long I replayed Slayer's allegations, remembered the Commissioner's bloody bedroom and his grieving wife.

Nothing made sense. No connection on why I'd kill him or why they suspected me of all people.

They'd made a huge mistake, and it was only a matter of time before they realized the truth.

Still, I sat there for who knew how long, ice threading through my veins, the chill numbing my brain. Up on my feet, I paced around to move and do something other than drowning in thoughts.

Yellow files layered the desk, I flicked through the numerous pages, most of the writing faded, the black and white photos washed out, corners chewed.

I drew open the drawer in a cabinet and plucked out a bunch of folders. Dozens of photos fell out and I poured over them, out of pure curiosity. So many old shots. Then my attention caught on a young girl with the greenest eyes and sandy hair that draped to her shoulders.

She looked so familiar. I lifted the photo to my face. She'd been the same girl Judas assumed was Bond's sister. I flipped through the folders and images, shoving them aside to reach the ones underneath until I finally tracked that black and white shot of the girl in a different shot. The first one showed her standing near the school woods, but in the second one, she wore jeans and was waving. In the distance... Wait. I squinted past the worn photo and studied the guy in the background.

"Bond?" It *was* him, with longer hair, but still, it was him.

He'd insisted she wasn't his sister before he stormed out of the tunnels last time we were down here. Was this girl someone else... someone special to him? Had she broken his heart?

The latter idea was poison in my veins. He'd been so angry when Judas raised the topic.

"Who are you?" I studied the photo and ran an index finger over her face, except a fire was flaring inside me that this blonde somehow still affected Bond so much after all this time. Maybe I was wrong, but I couldn't dampen the flames scorching my insides. He'd been so distant lately, vanishing when we needed him most.

No, he wouldn't do that to me. He couldn't. Would he? These photos were so old though. What was I missing?

I tossed the photo onto the pile and stumbled back to the couch before I slouched down and hugged myself. I didn't need to worry about that now... not when my world was dissolving around me. I rocked back and forth as heaviness dragged across my chest.

The hours flew past as I went over the events again and again for anything I'd missed. It continued to fly by that night, the next day, and another. Still, I remained clueless as to why Slayer had targeted me.

By the third night, I'd snuck into the girl's communal shower near the gymnasium to wash, and my stomach growled like a dragon for food, so once I dressed, I headed toward the cafeteria vending machines.

The moon hung low and pregnant overhead between black storm clouds, the Academy grounds transforming under the glimpse of moonlight into a silvery garden. A rumble rocked the heavens with the promise of a storm. Clouds slid over the moon again, and inky blackness sank over the land. I snuck through the shadows to avoid being seen by the CCTVs or anyone looking outside their windows so late at night, moving fast.

The crunch of a dead twig came from behind.

I shuddered as instinct took over, and I shoved myself behind a shrub, hunched low. I peered out between gaps in the branches to see who followed. The trees and bushes stood like silhouettes, the worn path stretching into the forest shone beneath the moon's gaze, and in those frozen seconds, fear skated down my arms.

The wind died. Leaves stopped rustling.

Slayer.

He'd found me, and I'd given myself away so easily. *Stupid, stupid, stupid.*

In a moment of complete stillness, a shadow appeared across the grounds, coming from the same direction I'd been seconds earlier. But he was too far away, and seeing who it was seemed impossible.

Hiding out on the Academy had been a mistake. I was torn and so confused about where to go next, but staying here wasn't the answer.

The figure moved with swiftness through the night and headed in the direction of the church.

A shudder ran through me. I'd been found. My hands trembled at my sides, and the moment he vanished from sight, I slipped out of the bushes and ran in the opposite direction, my gaze glued to the front gates of the Academy. Keeping my head low, I sprinted, leaving behind my clothes and bag and anything else I'd stuffed into my backpack. They didn't matter. Not now.

Drops of rain fell on my face, gentle at first, then sheets

of rain dropped from the heavens like someone had wrung out the clouds.

I was drenched in seconds, water running under my shirt and down my spine, slipping into my underwear. Its icy touch left me shivering. An attack of lighting flashed across the heavens, followed by the demented sounds of thunder cracking, shattering the peace.

I ran and ran, never stopping. I had no place to go, but stopping wasn't an option. The main building came into view, and I glanced behind me into the shadows, seeing no movement.

Iciness crawled up my back.

The rapid clap of footfalls over floorboards weren't lost beneath the pounding rain, and a figure emerged from the front of the main building.

I pivoted on my heels and darted toward a nearby tree that flanked the driveway of the Academy.

Water rolled down my face and neck in rivulets, and I clung to the tree, shaking and scared. Exhaustion wore me down, but I didn't budge an inch and watched the man rushing into his car. His movements were frantic and fast with one purpose—to get out of the rain. This wasn't the same figure I'd seen earlier on the grounds.

A flicker of light burst to life, carving through the darkness, illuminating the front gates. The hiss of tires on gravel found me as the black vehicle pulled onto the driveway.

Desperation rocked through me. I was alone, had nowhere to go, and was being hunted. There was nothing left to give. I swept the grounds with my gaze, not seeing anyone else, but despair clung to my ribs. I rubbed eyes that couldn't cry anymore and looked down at my shaking hands. They were wet and so freaking cold. Maybe I'd been a fool to think I could do this on my own.

The car moved closer and a sudden snap decision pierced my thoughts. I darted out of my hiding spot and stepped out in the path of the oncoming car. It skidded to a halt in front of me.

Blinded by the headlights, I stuck out a hand to block the lights.

Rain ran down my face, and I wanted to cry, but I was so tired and just needed a break. Something. Anything but interrogation.

He rolled down the window, his voice fighting the vicious storm. "Ms. Livingstone. We've been looking for you. Get in."

I took the lifeline he offered, rushing over and jumping into the passenger's seat.

Warmth cocooned around me in the car, while I dripped water everywhere. "Who's *we*," I asked, pulling at the seatbelt and strapping myself in.

He reached into the back and handed me a blanket, which I wrapped around me and used to dry my face. The prickly fabric scratched my skin, and I inhaled the smell of firewood and dog fur, but the blanket was warm and comforting.

"The Ancient and me," he explained before driving through the gate and past the Academy grounds. His gaze kept flicking to the mirror, checking if anyone followed.

"Vlad contacted you?" I slid lower in my seat, holding the blanket tight against me, shaking more from the dread of Slayer finding me than the cold rippling over my flesh.

"Heard it in passing that he summoned you."

My mind whirled. Did he want to ask if I killed the commissioner too?

Night swallowed the fields we passed, and I had no idea

where we were going. But it was away from whoever lurked on the school grounds.

He stabbed the buttons on his steering wheel and the phone rang through the car speakers.

"Hello?" Nefarious' voice had my ears perking.

"I apologize for the lateness of my call."

"Oh, okay." Nefarious paused and swallowed loudly. "I didn't even know that I gave you my number."

"You didn't. A package came for you today. One you've been looking for. You'll need to take it with you when you see the Ancient tomorrow." His voice remained monotonous, barren of emotions, and just like me, he hedged his bets that the detectives might be listening on his phone too and anyone in anyway associated with me.

"I wasn't planning on seeing the Ancient."

"You will...with the package. Meet me at Harvey's Accountants, and I'll deliver it there."

Radio silence. "Okay." Nefarious hung up.

We drove through the night, only the pelting sound of the rain assaulting the car accompanied us.

"Why are you helping me," I asked, turning in my seat, facing the Hellhound.

"Something's just not adding up with the allegations against you, and I want to give you the benefit of the doubt."

He didn't look over at me when he spoke, but his support was exactly what I needed right now. A safe haven and help as my world turned dark.

Cradled in the blanket, my spine pressed against the seat, I looked outside, and prayed to hell this mess with the commissioner's death was nothing more than a massive misunderstanding. Because if it wasn't... a whimper grazed my throat... I wasn't sure what I'd do.

CHAPTER FIVE

SAVING OR SIN?

I LOWERED MY HEAD AS THE ICY TRAIL OF WATER RAN down the back of my neck and under my shirt.

Balefire's car idled in the darkness further down the street. I could feel him watching me in the dark, waiting to get rid of the thorn in his side. I was a thorn...I was just a thorn who was desperate.

Headlights washed over me as I stood against the corner of the building. The lights bounced from the growing puddles as the car coasted along the darkened street and then turned. A bird called out behind me soft, urgent. I pressed harder against the building as the bird call came again.

Only it was too dark for birds to be out at this time...I turned my head catching movement through shoulder high sparse bushes.

"It's me," Nefarious whispered. "This way."

I turned back to the corner of the building, took a small step toward the pavement and nodded my head. In an instant the car rolled forward. Headlights blinded me as the nose of the car swung across the street. I turned, hurrying back into the darkness, and toward the movement as Nefarious came to my aid once more.

There was sadness as he met my gaze. "Morwenna…" he started.

"Please, Mr. Leathers, not now," I pleaded.

He flinched, and then gave a slow nod. I could only hope he understood how fragile I was, how I was barely holding myself together even as my stitching unraveled.

"Come on." He waved me forward. "Let's get you out of the rain."

I followed him through a narrow passageway beside an old abandoned house and a low set brick building. *Harvey's Accountants, making every dollar count,* was written across the front window.

"Just down here," Nefarious murmured and headed for a small navy hatchback parked further down the road.

He pressed the button and orange lights lit up the night as the *clunk* of a lock sounded. I rounded the car, scanned the streets and then climbed in. Nefarious had the car started and was pulling out into the night before I reached for my seatbelt. He glanced at me once more, taking in my sodden hair and wet clothes. "When we couldn't find you, I was sure something terrible had happened to you."

"Something terrible *has* happened to me." I lifted my head to meet his gaze.

I understood at that moment how isolated I truly was…when not even the Vampire sitting next to me could reach me. I glanced to the darkened streets as Nefarious drove forward and then pulled out into the street. I didn't take notice of where we went, or which part of the city he lived. Inside my head I was still in that interrogation room, still frozen to the chair as I stared at the images pinned to the board.

You'll slip up soon enough... Slayer's words filled my head. That same gnawing ache bloomed in my chest. Panic, that's what it was. I lowered my head and gripped the edge of the car seat. Pure panic. Pure...*desperation.* "Do you believe me?"

There was silence from my teacher. I lifted my head, finding his gaze in the dark. "Do you believe I killed the Commissioner?"

I didn't understand the need for him to believe me. Not when the events in my own mind were starting to scramble, and I was beginning to believe the lie.

"Yes," Nefarious answered. "I do believe you, but I also believe there's a reason you're being singled out, and I'm not sure if you're an innocent party to it all."

To it all? "Are you saying I'm somewhat responsible?"

"Yes," he answered. "I am."

He turned the car into a side street and stopped in a darkened alley between a sex club and what looked like an old forgotten church. "Where are we?"

"My home." He killed the engine and climbed out. "Here I have the best of both worlds, what are you in need of Morwenna? Saving, or Sin?"

I flinched with his words, and slowly reached for the door handle, yanked and then climbed out, stepping into a puddle.

"Through here," Nefarious called and strode toward the only gate in the middle of a concrete wall. He hit the remote, locking the car as he pulled a bolt backwards and swung the gate wide.

I followed, mostly because I had no other option.

"Just swing the gate shut. Won't be long until we leave anyway."

Leave? My hand stilled on the wet wooden slats. Oh,

that's right...the Ancient. I inhaled hard and stepped through the gate, turning long enough to latch it closed. Nefarious' steps rang out on the pavement. I followed, my mind a whirlwind of lies and murder. I was many things, a liar, a manipulator, but not a murderer...not like they said.

I lifted my gaze to the dark silhouette of my teacher and climbed the path that led to a small door in the towering building.

"Watch where you step," he called over his shoulder. "Some of the floor is rotten, you'll fall right through."

I was careful, making sure to step where he stepped. Still the wooden floor howled and groaned under my weight as I lingered long enough to close the door behind me. "Are you renovating?"

"No." He gave a shrug and strode through a hallway before hitting a switch.

A soft amber bulb gave me just enough light to see by.

"I like the feel of the bare bones of this place. It serves me well, and no one bothers to break in."

He kept to the edge, rounding the base of a set of stairs and then climbed. I kept to the left, glancing at the hole on the right hand side of the floor and gripped the banister, climbing the first stair and then higher.

"I've got some clothes that might come close to fitting you. They'll keep you warm while I wash and dry what you have on. Have you eaten?" He stilled at the question, one foot on the stair above and looked down.

I shook my head. "I'm not hungry."

"Suit yourself," he continued to climb and then strode along the landing.

This wasn't the warm welcome I'd expected, and yet what had been in the last seventy-two-hours of madness that was my life. But I had no choice, not in any of this.

No, I did have a choice. It's just I was forced to make this one.

I steeled my spine and followed him along the landing and into a room. Nefarious was busy grabbing clothes from a drawer, his attention elsewhere. I saw him now, saw him for who he truly was. He wouldn't go to battle for me, no more than Balefire would. But those who would were the ones I needed to protect the most.

I reached into my pocket and gripped my phone. *Love and miss you already.* The message was still waiting for me to respond, and as much as it hurt to stand there while my heart was breaking—this was the choice I made.

"This should be good." Nefarious turned and held out the clothes in his hand.

I wanted to meet his gaze. I wanted to ask him when exactly the tide had turned for me...was it with the Diamond's or Slayer? After all, he blamed me. I could see it in the way he refused to meet my eyes.

"Thank you," I murmured and took what he offered.

I would. I'd take it all. I understood now.

I was the monster they feared.

"There's a bathroom down the hall. You can change there while I gather my things. The Ancient doesn't like to wait."

I gave a nod, grasped the clothes and then strode from the room. I found the small run down bathroom at the end of the hall, switched on the light and then turned to face the chipped mirror above the cracked ceramic sink.

Dark eyes, sodden flat hair. There was a stranger in the glass. A stranger who stared back with a shell-shocked gaze. I reached up, pressed fingers to my cheek. One nail was chipped, dirt welled under another. "This isn't me." The words slipped from my lips. "This isn't Morwenna Livingstone."

"Morwenna, are you talking to someone?" Nefarious called from outside the bathroom.

Was he listening to me?

"No," I answered and straightened. "Just myself."

"The Ancient—"

"Doesn't like waiting, *yeah I got it.*" I grasped the black hoodie and yanked it over my head before I shed the t-shirt underneath.

Sneakers and my jeans were next. The wet denim slapped the floor as I shoved them free. I grasped a clean towel from a dresser and wiped the moisture from my body. Maybe the Ancient knew something I didn't. Maybe he could guide me...*maybe even hide me.*

I stilled, my hand on my belly and lifted my head. *He didn't like waiting...was that code for something?* I lowered my arm and glanced to the door. Was that why Nefarious was being so standoffish?

In his own home, though? *Unless we were being listened to...*

Maybe the place was bugged?

The more I thought of it, the more I was convinced that's what was happening. Slayer and the mortal detectives weren't just content with lying and manipulating to get what they wanted...they were willing to bug houses too.

I hurried, yanking on the black t-shirt and oversized hoodie, and then lifted the black cargo pants, looking at the shape and the size. They were a woman's, the thought of wearing Nefarious' lover's clothes made my skin crawl. But right now I couldn't afford to be picky.

I yanked on the pants, and stepped back into my soaked sneakers. The floorboards groaned outside the door as I grabbed my clothes from the floor and yanked open the door.

His eyes widened as I rushed from the room, and then lowered to the pants he gave me. "I'm glad they fit, they were my sisters, Helena."

I caught my breath as surprise gripped me. "Yes, thank you."

His every word was careful, every movement as well. With a nod he held out his hand, taking the drenched clothes from me. "I'll put these in the wash and we can go."

I followed him down the stairs to the crumbling lower floor, and hovered at the base of the stairs while he disappeared through a door that led to a sparkling white kitchen. I followed, for no other reason than to try to understand this man.

The kitchen was perfect, an old cast iron sink, brass pots hanging from hooks overhead. The rush of water started with the hum of a washing machine as Nefarious stepped inside, and then lifted his head. "Oh, you're there."

"It's beautiful." I glanced around the room.

"And it was all designed by my mother."

I realized I really didn't know Nefarious Leathers at all. "Your Mom?"

He nodded, taking a step toward the sink to rearrange a washcloth. "Father was a preacher, Mom was... Well, she wasn't one to wait while he chased any young woman that asked for absolution. So Mom went and found herself a companion for the night, taking me with her. Only he was after a lot more than her company...he also wanted her blood."

I flinched. "Your maker?"

One nod was all that was needed. "And that, as they

say, is that. We'd better get going." He motioned for the doorway.

We followed the same path we'd taken coming in, keeping to the stairs as we made our way to the door at the end of the rectory. It was a weird looking church. The living quarters stretching out behind the church itself.

I left it all behind, stepping back out into the night. The heady scent of rain hung in the air. I made my way down the path to the locked gate. When I grabbed it, the hinges squealed and the gate swung free.

"I locked this when I came through." I turned, glancing at Nefarious. "You saw me."

He made no move to acknowledge anything, just motioned toward the car. "We can't keep the Ancient waiting."

Yellow lights blinked as the car unlocked. My footsteps echoed, mingling with the slow thud of Nefarious' stride. I glanced over my shoulder, scanning the shadows before I climbed into the car.

The Ancient would know what to do. I knew that now. *I hoped more likely.*

A chill swept down my spine as I reached for the handle of the door. Nefarious yanked open his door as I climbed inside.

"Are you ready?" he said. "Ready to go and see the Ancient once more?"

I gave a nod, even though I knew he couldn't see it in the dark.

I trembled, the pressure building inside me like a breath that was caught...and I knew I wouldn't find release, not until this was over. *Not until I saw the Ancient.*

CHAPTER SIX

FALLING DEEPER

THE ANCIENT'S MANSION LIVED UNDER A CONSTANT shadow, as if the sun reached for walls that kept shrinking away from its rays. Windows were blacked out by curtains, and paint flakes lined the frames like they'd been there for centuries. Everything about his double-story home screamed haunted mansion. From the wrought iron gates at the front of the property, to the ivy clinging to the stone walls and curling around the colossal structure.

I glanced over my shoulder as Nefarious parked down the street under a weeping tree. He insisted on waiting for me outside when I asked if he'd come inside too. While I stood at the front door and chewed on my lower lip, I could only assume his royal Ancient Vampness had summoned me to discuss recent events with Slayer.

Reaching over, I grasped the round, brass knocker and banged it several times, the sound reminding me of fireworks detonating.

The shuffle of steps closed in from inside. "Hang on," a deep voice called out.

So I waited and patted down my wind-blown hair,

never quite sure if I ought to dress a certain way when meeting with Vlad.

The grand wooden door slid open to a figure lingering in the shadows inside the home, but his pale face and red eyes told me exactly who stood there.

"Your grace." I bent at the waist, giving him a bow, lowering my head in respect as I'd seen Dad do many times.

"Come in then. Quickly." He broke into a cough and stepped aside, waving me in.

I stepped into a darkened hallway, the Ancient was already staggering down a corridor before vanishing into a side room. Quick to shut the door behind me, I trailed after him, right into his bedroom.

Halting in the doorway, I watched him climb into a king poster bed with black sheets, his arms and legs shaking as he did. The window shutters were drawn and only a lamp on the bedside table illuminated the room, tossing a yellow tinge across the treasure box located at the foot of the bed and the paintings peppering the walls. They were of people at a ball in fancy gowns and elaborate wigs.

The Ancient coughed and I realized that he looked thinner, smaller.

"Are you feeling all right?" I asked. As an Ancient, he was one of a few Vamps who retained strong abilities such as turning into mist, but right now he was frail.

"Haven't felt well since I touched those cursed Diamonds." He broke into another fit of coughs, and I couldn't help but feel guilty. Even if it hadn't been my fault exactly.

"What can I do to help?" I pushed into the room, the heavy stench of sickness and perspiration smothering me. He no longer resembled the strong, intimidating Vampire

I'd encountered that night when I'd shown him the Diamonds.

"Blood tea, child," he murmured, drawing the blankets up to his chin. He hacked his lungs out again, sounding like a barking dog, and waved for me to go, pointing to the hall.

So, I swung around and rushed down the darkened corridor, passing closed doors until I reached the kitchen on my left. Inside, the walls were white while the counter, chandelier, and every appliance was in black, and the pots and pans were a deep violet. The Ancient had planned out his kitchen, even if he wouldn't do a lot of cooking; he had every gadget. He even had a knife holder in the shape of a coffin. Gaudy, but then Vlad wasn't exactly the typical Vamp either.

I opened the cupboard doors, finding so many plates and bowls and cups. I grabbed a black mug with the words, *Voodoo Potion,* and kept checking everywhere for tea. Finding nothing in the top shelves, I went through the drawers to find elaborate cutlery. He barely had any food aside from a few crackers, yet he was set up for hosting parties.

In the last drawer, I finally tracked down some lemon tea bags. Mom had made this drink for me growing up when I didn't feel well. Inside the fridge were two bags of blood O type, so I grabbed one, eyeing the slice of blood cake, figuring he'd notice if I took a bite.

I shoved the fridge door shut, when a figure stumbled into the doorway.

I flinched and rocked back into the counter, my body shuddering. "Shit!"

A tall, lanky man dressed in a hoodie and jeans blocked the doorway. "I didn't expect *you* in the kitchen," he muttered, his eyes wide and just as startled as me.

"What are you doing here? Who are you?" Panic sliced through me that Slayer was somehow connected to him, that the henchman would round the corner and come for me.

"I-I'm Vlad's blood donor," he stammered, his voice unstable, filled with nerves. His arms hung limp by his sides, his fingers flexing, and I saw the bruises marring his knuckles like he'd been punching something hard.

"You have a key to the house?"

His kept glancing down the hallway and back at me, and each time he turned I caught the glimmer of three blue dots along his neck, lit up from under his skin—the latest trend in tattoos.

"He let me in earlier. I'm just waiting until he's ready."

I stiffened, a sense of uncertainty fogging my thoughts because he must have seen me come into the house, watched me, maybe even listened to my conversation with Vlad. If the Ancient still took fresh blood from the vein, then maybe the bag of blood I clutched belonged to this donor.

"What are you looking for?" I asked, curious why he looked so nervous.

"Bathroom." He lowered his head and vanished down the hall.

Something about this felt wrong, like how could he not know where the bathroom is? So, I tiptoed to the hall and stared out to find this donor peering into the Ancient's room before he headed toward the next room, gripping his ribs on his right hand side. Whoever he fought had gotten some good hits.

Strange, though, being a new donor had to be nerve-wracking, especially if feeding an Ancient. I returned to the kitchen, filled the electric kettle with water, and switched it on. I kept checking the hallway, but the guy didn't return. I poured the boiled water on the teabag, filling only a third of the cup and jiggled the tea for two minutes. Then broke the seal on the blood bag and topped it into the mug. A quick stir of the tea and I took two quick mouthfuls of the blood from the bag, the metallic aroma making me salivate. I set the bag in the fridge and carried the cup into the bedroom.

"Just met your donor," I murmured as the Ancient pulled himself to a sitting position.

He reached for the cup with shaky hands and pressed the edge to his lips before slurping. A quick lick of his lips and his shoulders sagged in exaggerated relief.

"Perfect." He glanced over at me, his stare intense despite his weakening body. "He's the regular. Mike is always a jumpy young human."

I nodded, not getting the impression Mike was the regular. If he fed the Ancient, why'd he spy on him earlier or not know where the bathroom was, and why be so jumpy at seeing me?

I pulled a seat closer to the bed before sliding into it. "You wanted to see me." My knees kept bouncing, and something about Mike in the house made me uncomfortable, especially since I was trying to keep a low profile.

Vlad took another mouthful before setting the cup down on the bedside table. "Your power is strong for such a young Vampire. But you need to be careful. Your friends and family are in grave danger. We're all in danger." Weariness crossed his expression and something I'd never expected to see in the eyes of the powerful Vlad now flooded his gaze.

Fear.

He was scared.

And it deepened the terror already clinging to my insides.

"What do you mean?" I fumbled with the hem of my shirt while dread looped around me until there was no room for anything else. "Danger?" I knew the answer... It was etched across my brain, but I had to be sure and hear the words from Vlad.

"These are dangerous times for all of us, and I'm not as strong as I used to be." He reached for his cup and gulped the blood tea, but he didn't elaborate right away, so I waited. Grilling an Ancient would most likely get me kicked out of his house, but I needed to know if he could help me. Maybe I had it all wrong... maybe all he worried about was his own frail body.

"Child, I'll try my best to protect you, but you need to stay hidden. You must stay safe and keep your distance from those who'd harm us."

I inched to the edge of my seat, gripping the armrests, swallowing hard. He had to know the truth, and I waited for his suggestion on how to help keep me protected.

His lips pursed, and something darkened his expression. "I think I made a mistake giving you the role of Understudy."

An ache settled in the middle of my chest, my brain on fire as my thoughts melted together into a pool of conflicting emotions. "I'm doing my best." But as the words fell from my mouth, I regretted them, and how weak it made me sound. My mind flew to Dad, and I already I pictured his disappointment when he found out I'd lost the position.

"I don't think... I know," he reaffirmed, and this response cut through me. His voice was dark and cold, and my throat thickened. "You don't think things through, like how you allowed the Sewer Dweller into your room and he released the curse of the Diamonds."

"That wasn't my fault."

"Just focus on staying safe and nothing else," he hissed.

My muscles flexed as his sucker punch left me stunned. But with it came the reminder that everything in my life was falling apart.

"I can do this." I raised my voice, and he jerked his attention to me, his mouth twisting into a grimace.

"I never make a decision lightly," he snapped.

I wanted to just get up and leave and not hear him remind me how I'd failed. I had enough crap in my world right now reminding me of that.

Up on my feet, I tugged on my shirt and tilted my head up, pushing away the doubts creeping in.

"I'll show myself out." Nothing I could say would change his mind, and if I was forced to fight this alone, then I'd do it and prove them all wrong.

The Ancient just studied me, didn't way a word, and I marched out of his room, tears pricking my eyes.

I couldn't rely on him, but I'd show him and the humans how wrong they'd been. No matter what it took, I'd figure out who killed the Commissioner and clear my name.

A flash of movement caught my eye near the doorway. Mike! I rushed forward and found him gone. Had he been listening to our conversation?

To my left, a nearby door sat slightly ajar. I crept closer before peering inside to see him at the window, behind the curtain, staring intently at something in the front yard.

I retreated and reached for the front door before pulling it open. A cold breeze curled around my body, blowing hair into my face. Shutting the door, I looked outside to an empty yard. Beyond the gates, Nefarious stood outside his car in plain view of the window in the side room.

Why would Mike spy on Nefarious? Maybe not even the Ancient was as safe as he thought he was? The reminder that I was on the run struck hard. For all I knew, Mike worked for Slayer.

I pushed into a run across the yard and past the front gates. "Get in the car," I called out to Nefarious. "We need to leave now!"

CHAPTER SEVEN

SWITZERLAND

"Stop the car." I stared into the darkness.

"What?" Nefarious cut a glare my way. "Why?"

*You know why...*The thought filled my head but of course I couldn't say it out loud. "I just need some air," I murmured.

The *tick...tick...tick...*of the turn signal filled the space. Nefarious glanced into the rear view mirror and then eased the car onto the shoulder of the road. The pent up tension in me seemed to spill outwards like ripples on a pond. My fingers shook, reaching for the handle of the door, and my thighs quaked as I pushed free.

I had no idea what I was doing, but then again, that seemed to somehow fit with the way my life was unravelling. Cold night air still held the promise of another downpour. Gravel crunched as I stepped to the side and then closed the door.

"You okay?" Nefarious followed, stepping out with me.

"I will be," I answered and then started walking.

This time I didn't stop. Bathed in the headlights of my teacher's car, I kept walking.

"Morwenna," Nefarious called behind me.

"Don't wait up, Mr. Leathers," I called into the night, as I strode toward the sparkling lights of Tricks City. "I won't be home anytime soon."

Even though I was leaving everything I knew behind, I exhaled that pent up emotion...and lengthened my stride. Headlights washed over me a few minutes later. Nefarious slowed for a second and fear reached from the pit in my stomach. For one horrible second I envisioned him stopping the car, dragging me back inside. Would he take me back to the police station? Back to Slayer and the mortal detectives who waited with white clothes in hand, ready to lock me away?

Until they figured out a cell was no good for someone like me—I'd live forever. I walked until that image was burned inside my head. I walked until it faded...I walked until *I faded,* and there was just the motion.

Cars whipped past on the highway before I turned down a familiar road. The dark skies brightened overhead. I waited for the first glimpse of sunrise, but none came. Grey filled my world, and a light splattering of rain smacked my cheek. I lowered my head, striding past the cross roads where I'd stood with Judas and the Wolves.

The faint hum of power lingered in my chest. I lifted my hand, fingers probing against the bone. For all the power I'd held in this body...I felt powerless now. I felt less than powerless...*I felt mortal.*

Street lights hummed, but no cars drove here, no blare of horns, no thumping music. It was *empty.* Void. But the more I walked, the better I felt. Step by step, the belts were unbuckling...and there was only the core of me left.

I lifted my head as the grey sky grumbled overhead and my gaze lingered on the towering outline of the Blood Moon

Coven. I hadn't consciously made the decision to come here. Just like the remnant of power that lingered inside, I was drawn to the power of this place. The closer I came the more I realised this place somehow knew me too.

And it wasn't the only one.

The front door opened and a Warlock strode out. Only this Warlock I knew. *This* Warlock had been a welcoming party for me before.

"Morwenna," Keir murmured and flicked the lighter in his hand. "We've been expecting you."

He turned then, giving me his back. I supposed that was a better reception than I'd hoped for. At least this time there were no secrets, no lies. This time my father didn't wait in the basement chained like a beast. I strode along the pavement and slowly climbed the stairs.

The sky gave one last snarl of warning before the rain started again. I whispered a *thank you,* and strode across the landing to the open door.

The place was exactly as I remembered it, dust-choked and creepy. The rooms were so sparsely furnished that our footsteps rang out like gunshots. I felt the tremble in the floorboards, like the vibration had a song of its own.

"Tagar," I started.

"He knows you're here, like I said, we've been expecting you."

Hope whispered in my ear, but I couldn't listen to it, not yet, not when there was too much at stake. I followed the Warlock as he flicked the lighter, casting a glint of amber flame into the shadows before snuffing out the light again. We made our way along an unfamiliar hallway to a set of stairs.

My sneakers squealed as we climbed. A voice rang out above us somewhere, and in the echo, another voice made itself known. Shadows shifted around me as I hit the first floor and kept climbing. Soft chants rang out, and the sharp smell of citrus and black pepper pinched my nose.

"Morning prayers," Keir muttered without turning his head to look at me.

They weren't the words I waited for. I'd readied myself for accusations, prepared myself to plead my innocence, even from someone I barely knew, like Keir. Yet there was nothing but silence as we climbed past the second floor to the third.

"Last door on the right, knock three times exactly and enter." He motioned toward a door at the far end of the hall. "And it's good to see you, Morwenna. Good to feel the connection to the Mother once more."

He left me then, flicking his lighter as he turned on his heel and descended the stairs.

*Flick...flick...flick...*I listened to the sound of Keir leaving, and then turned my attention to the end of the hall. There was no light under the door. Maybe there was no one inside?

A tremble rippled from the middle of my chest, like the soft touch of a finger, and that pull inside me became a little bolder. I took a step, leaving the stairs behind and made my way toward the door.

Knock three times, Keir was insistent on that.

I lifted my hand, clenched my fist and quietly rapped on the door. The brass handle twisted in front of me, and the door swung inwards. There was no one on the other side. No one waiting... No one hiding. It was just me.

I turned and looked over the balcony as Keir disappeared into the hallway, leaving me behind. "This is the right door. Knock three times, he said," I muttered and then pushed the door wider.

There was a seat on one side and a desk on the other. Blood red velvet curtains rippled against the far wall. I stepped inside, not really wanting to close the door behind me, until a low, soft voice came from behind the curtain. "You don't have to be afraid of me, Morwenna."

Tagar Lutherian stepped out from around the edge of the crimson curtain, and strode toward the center of the room. "Sit." He motioned to the chair and then took in my disheveled appearance. "I'll have some hot tea brought to you. Have you eaten?"

I shook my head.

"Very well," he answered. "A blood shake too."

He was just like I'd seen him last, poised, *regal*. But underneath, there was sadness. I was sure when others looked at him all they saw was power, but all I saw was a heartbroken man spending the rest of eternity in mourning.

"Thank you," I answered and took the seat in front of his desk.

Black and white images filled the corner of his desk. The smiling face of a young woman...a young witch actually. Willow stared back at me. Tagar was there too, smiling, his spine ram-rod straight, with his arm wrapped around her. He looked proud and in love. But that was another time, back when he called himself by another name, back before Willow attacked him and she was killed in self-defense.

Now he was a High Priest of the Blood Moon Coven, and my only hope....

"I'm guessing you've heard," I started, and then swallowed hard. Hell, this was harder than I thought. "I didn't do it. I didn't kill the Commissioner."

"I know," he answered a matter of fact. "Even if you did,

it wouldn't change my decision of allow you within these walls."

I flinched as his words sank in. "It wouldn't, why?"

"I owe you a debt I can never repay," he said sullenly. "I'm not talking about breaking the curse." He glanced to the images of the witch he was to marry. "You bought her peace, and that is why I don't care if you murdered the Commissioner. I wouldn't care if you murdered the whole corrupt line. You require a safe haven? The Blood Moon Academy is yours."

I sank against the back of the chair. Just like that? No interrogations? No promises, no pleading for my damn life? I looked down, as the weight of everything came crashing around me.

My voice trembled, and then shattered. "Thank you. Thank you so much. I didn't mean to bring this to your door. But I had nowhere else to go, nowhere they haven't already bugged or have been watching. Nowhere that was *safe*."

"Well." Tagar lifted the handle on his phone and pressed it to his ear. "The Blood Moon Coven is safe. Think of us as Switzerland." The person on the other end of the line answered, and he quickly gave an order for a blood shake and hot tea before hanging up.

"How safe?" I glanced to the images. He didn't need more chaos in his life.

"Are you worried for yourself, or for us?"

I'd be a liar if I wasn't thinking about myself. "Mostly for the students. I don't want them attacked, or bugged....or threatened."

Tagar pressed his spine into his chair, his lips curving into a smile. "They're not going to attack us, Morwenna. They *certainly* are not going to threaten us. I'm not sure if you've noticed, but the supernatural kind doesn't take too kindly to us Witches. They're afraid of us. *Everyone* is afraid of us."

"Even Slayer?" The words slipped free before I knew. Once they were out there, it was too late to silence *his* name.

Tagar clasped his hands in front of his body and met my gaze. "Is that who's after you? I'd heard rumors...but I wasn't sure."

"Yes," That single word was all I could manage.

Silver eyes stared at me from the darkness of my mind.

"If he's involved that means you're in more danger than we thought. I'm glad you came, Morwenna. I'm glad that we can protect you. You have to find a way to clear your name. You *have to* find a way to get Slayer off your trail, anyway you can."

There were three deafening knocks at the door. With a quick wave of his hand, and a wince, Tagar released a flicker of power. The door opened inwards, and heavy steps crossed the floor.

"Crimsyn," he muttered, and then sighed.

"You expect me to wait on you like a damn servant?" She snarled without looking at me once. "The next time you'll eat the goddamn food I bring, tray and all."

He closed his eyes for a moment, and then slowly lifted his hand. "The food was an added bonus, I thought there was someone you should see."

Only then did she turn and look at me, and the wild Hearth Witch I knew smiled. "Mor?" she muttered, and then looked at my wet hair and dirty clothes. "What the fuck."

"What the fuck, indeed." Tagar gave his hand a wave and door to his study closed again

Crimsyn and Tagar had a complicated relationship, but seeing them together like this made me smile. "I'm surprised you're here," I murmured. "The most vivid words of yours I can remember are...*I'm not interested in going to your stupid fucking Academy. So do me a favor and piss off.*"

"Yeah well..." she muttered, with a snarl. "Things change."

"She means money," Tagar muttered under his breath, and then lifted his gaze. "But we are *very* happy Crimsyn has finally realised Blood Moon is where she needs to be."

"You know one day you'll say it like you damn well mean it. *Anyway,* I'm glad to see you. I'm taking the blood shake is yours?" She reached over, grasped the tall green glass from the tray and passed it to me. "Why are you here? And why do you look like Hell?"

I took a sip of the shake, letting the taste of pennies slide down the back of my throat before I started. "You wouldn't believe me if I told you."

"And *that,* is my cue to leave. Lock up the study when you're done, Crimsyn. I trust you can take care of whatever Morwenna needs."

"Morwenna, you're perfectly safe here. No one will get through our wards, no one who means you harm that is. Eat, rest, come to me if you need anything at all. Crimsyn." He gave a small nod of his head.

The Witch just curled her top lip and stared him down until, with a sigh, he strode from his own damn study and closed the door.

"Good to see you two getting along," I muttered and sipped the shake.

"Yeah, well. The cottage went beserk after the Witch storm and burned itself to the damn ground, along with all my belongings, so it wasn't like I had a choice. Anyway..."

She sat her ass on the edge of the desk, and turned her focus on me. "Enough about me. Tell me what's happened. Don't tell me Great...Great...Great Aunt Willow is causing you trouble again?"

"I never thought I'd say this, but I'd rather Demons and dark, powerful Witches any day of the week than this."

"Tell me," she urged. "Tell me everything."

I didn't want to start at the beginning. I mean, where was the beginning? Did it start with the Vampires at my 100th birthday, or did it start when they came for me? I started talking, and the words just kept coming. The horror, the hate, the Commissioner's wife. I still couldn't get her screams out of my head, or the way her nails stung my skin.

Crimsyn just sat there in silence as the tale became darker and darker and darker.

Until I murmured, "I found him there, Crimsyn, spying on the Ancient, listening to me. There's no place I can hide, there's no one I could turn to—except the Witches...except here."

"Jesus Christ in a ham sandwich," she whispered, her eyes wide and round. "You are in deep shit my friend."

"Tell me something I don't know."

"So, how are you gonna get yourself out of it?" She pushed off the desk to stand.

"I wish I knew," I murmured, staring at a spot on the desk.

"Well, like Tagar said, you're safe here. But we need to keep you here, so how about a room and all the hot water you can handle?"

I shoved up from the seat. "That sounds so damn good. I'd say that I would kill for a shower and about ten hours of uninterrupted sleep, but I don't want to push my luck."

"You are one weird Vampire," Crimsyn murmured and shook her head.

She shoved off the desk and made for the door. I left the glass and the hot tea behind. Weariness weighed me down. It wasn't just the need for sleep, it was for silence. I needed time to think, to plan how to fix this, and stay alive.

We walked out of the study and back down the stairs to the second level. I wanted to ask her questions, where she stayed...if she liked being here, and where on earth were all the students? Instead, I gripped the bannister and followed as she turned right, and cut across the landing.

The Blood Moon Academy wasn't like Bestias. Students rooms were all in the one main building. But there were hallways upon hallways, like a damn maze. I glanced over my shoulder and looked back the way we'd come.

"Here you go, back of the building away from all the noise." She stepped up to the door, but didn't open it right away.

Instead she leaned close to the wood, and held her hand over the handle. Whispered words weren't meant for my ears, but I had an idea what she was doing. The door would be enchanted only for me, or anyone who came to my aid, and in a second she lowered her hand, gripped the handle and the turned. "Home, sweet home." Crimsyn stepped inside and flicked on the light.

I would've slept on a mattress on the floor. But I was grateful for a sturdy single bed against the wall on one side, and a small desk on the other. The bathroom was smaller than the one at Bestias, but it was clean and neat.

"I'll rustle you up clothes and another shake. The curtains are heavy lined, so you'll be able to sleep like the dead."

I cut her a look.

"Sorry, you know what I mean. Anyway, come find me if you need someone to talk to. My room is four doors down and I barely sleep in this place. I think it's noise. I miss the quiet of the Moors."

With a small smile she turned and left, and once again I was alone. I moved toward the door, closing it behind her, and pressed my palm on the wooden frame. I could feel the power humming in the grain. "You'll protect me, won't you?"

I couldn't believe I was asking a damn door to keep me safe. But nothing in my life was sane anymore. A soft knock came from the other side of the door. I flinched, caught the shadows shift as someone bent, left something on the ground and then walked away. I counted to ten, and then opened. There was a pile of clothes, some towels, and a small bag of toiletries. A note stuck to the top. *Witches take care of their own.*

I'd never been so grateful in that moment. Never felt so humble, so broken down and grateful for this pile of clothes and cheap shampoo. I reached down, grasped the jeans, the hoodie, the soap and the note and stood. The paper trembled in my grasp. I glanced along the hallway to where the footsteps had faded. "Thank you," I whispered. "For everything."

I hurried back into my room and locked the door as the world around me shimmered behind fresh tears. I promised myself I wouldn't cry, that crying was being defeated, but in this moment there was no stopping the torrent that ran down my cheeks.

I held onto that note and wept. I wept for my family, and my friends. I wept for the Commissioner and his wife, but I refused to weep for me. There would be not one tear for me. Not one. I swallowed the lump in the back of my throat and made my way to the bed before I kicked my sneakers free.

A shower and sleep. All the tears in the world would have to wait. I was finding a way out of this mess...even if it took me the rest of my life. I carried the toiletries into the bathroom, stripped the grimy clothes from my body and turned on the shower.

Heat pummelled my skin. I tilted my head backwards, letting the spray wash through my hair before I scrubbed everything clean and then ended the spray.

I felt like I'd lived a thousand years as I stepped from the shower and grabbed a towel. I dried with slow, weak movements and then stepped out into the bedroom.

*Tink...tink...tink...*three hard taps came at the window. I hurried, yanking on the clothes before I neared the heavy drapes. No one knew I was here...no one *should know I was here.* My heart gave a hard *thump* and the echo of fear raced through my body.

I stepped toward the end of the window as a *tink...tink...*came once more. Hard jagged breaths filled me. Bare feet were soft on the floor. I gripped the edge of the heavy drape and opened. I could see no one, until they stepped backwards.

A young woman bent and picked something from the ground, tested the weight in her hand before she lifted her head.

Our gaze connected, brown eyes and a mess of brown tangled hair. She stilled, with the small pebble in her hand and waited. Hope raged in her eyes.

Huntleigh Blackthorne was the last person I'd expected to see...

CHAPTER EIGHT

NOT THE WOLF I WAS EXPECTING

Huntleigh dropped the pebble in her hand and motioned with her fingers as she mouthed the words, *open the window*. I stilled, not sure...and yet the wards on this room were strong. But they were for the door, weren't they? Not for the windows.

Morwenna, she mouthed my name. *I know you don't trust me. But I want to help you. Let me in.*

My stomach tightened, exhaustion called me. I glanced at the bed, feeling the pull of slumber...but the faces in my head were relentless. Judas. Nero. Bond. Ava. Chuck. I reached up, yanked open the latch and felt the cold wind cut through the room.

"Step back," Huntleigh called.

The curtains flapped as I followed her command. She reached up, gripped the straps of her pack, took three giants steps backwards and focused on the sill.

She was seamless, flawless, bounding across the sodden leaves before she lunged into the air. Her boots smacked the side of the building. Two floors off the ground was no match for a Wolf. She reached through the opening, heaved her leg through the window and then tumbled silently to the ground.

She sucked in a breath, brushed her wild hair from her face and then straightened. Brown eyes glinted with silver as she shifted her stance, taking in the sparse room and the neatly made bed. "Nice."

"What are you doing here, Huntleigh?" I muttered.

I could see the cogs turning inside her mind as she searched my gaze, searching for what to say. "I'm probably the last person you expected to see, right?"

"I'm really tired, I'm sorry but I can't do this right now. I need to sleep, and I need to think."

"And figure out who's doing this?" Her words were careful as she shifted her stance once more.

I didn't trust her, this Wolf, even if she was Judas' cousin. The one and only time I had anything to do with her was when we were forced together as partners for a class on instinct. My instinct was screaming right now, just watching her.

And it wasn't saying anything good.

"You don't know me," she continued. "Hell, my own family doesn't even know me. But I can help you track the people who're behind this. I can help you take them down."

She knew.

She knew it all.

I didn't know how, or why. But that's what I could see in her eyes, behind the pretense, and the lies. *No,* that voice whispered in the back of my mind. She can't know. I never told her. I never told anyone. Was she here for Judas? Was she his spy, trying to work out if I was the one bending the truth?

If that was the case then I had to be careful. Lucifer below, I had to be so careful. The thought of those I love being hunted by the Slayer sent a cold shiver along my spine. I had to keep them away from all of this. I had to protect them at all costs.

I knew that from the beginning.

"I don't know what you mean. I told Judas..."

"You told Judas a lie. You know it. *I know it.* I even know why." She shrugged the pack from her shoulders.

That chill from my spine raced outwards until all I felt was the bitter grip of fear. "I don't know what you're talking about."

She turned from me then, giving a shrug of defiance and strode around the room. "Whatever."

Annoyance crept closer. "Like I said, I'm tired."

"You think it's the bodyguard, right? I mean, if I were you, I'd think it was the bodyguard. That spill of blood was no nick of the finger. He did a good job cleaning it up." She curled her fingers and stared at her nails. "But no amount of cleaning can cover it completely, short of burning the cottage down. That's on the cards I suppose."

I flinched, panicked breath spilling. Sleep was falling away now, into the anger. "Are you threatening me? Is that why you're here?"

She said nothing, not even when I closed the distance between us and grabbed her arm. One yank until she met my gaze. "You threaten him again—"

"Slayer is after you," she snarled. Hate glinted in her eyes, trapped under that shine of steel. "He's here, he's come for you, and you are all on your own."

I stilled, sucked in a hard breath, my fingers still digging into sinewy muscles. "What the fuck did you day."

"I know it's the Council. I know it's a trap, just one more step up the ladder for them. They're using you, Mor."

"Morwenna," I snarled. "Only my friends call me Mor."

Her arm jumped in my grip as she shrugged once more. "Won't matter soon anyway. You'll have no friends left, because you'll be locked away in a cell, or worse, you'll be gone."

There was a flicker of something then, panic, *terror*. She was hiding something from me. I didn't trust her...seemed the feeling was mutual.

I dropped my hold on her arm. "How do I know I can trust you?"

For the first time she spoke the truth. "You can't. That's the thing, that's what *they* want you to believe. They want you running, they want you scared." She came closer, until I could pin-point every tiny freckle across her nose. "But what they don't want is you thinking...and figuring this shit out on your own."

Figuring it out.

Figuring it all out.

I could still see the mortal's fear when I found him spying on me and the Ancient. Still smell his terror, still taste his pain. I'd been running. I'd been hiding. I'd been trying to piece this mess together inside my head, but it was impossible...on my own.

I looked at her then, searched her eyes for meaning. "Do you think I killed the Commissioner?"

"No." The answer was instant. There was no thinking, no calculating. Just...*no.* "I don't."

I stepped away from her and stumbled toward the bed.

"So what are you going to do, *Morwenna?* Are you going to cower and hide, or are you going to figure it out? Who killed the Commissioner? Who had the means to murder him on one of the most well protected streets in Tricks City, and why are they framing you for the job?"

She was right. Every word, every *terrifying* word.

Movement crowded the edges of my view as she stepped closer. "What are you gonna do, Mor? Tell me that...*what are you gonna do?*"

"I'm going to figure it out." I lifted my gaze, meeting that silver glare. "I'm going find out who did this and why."

Her lips curled into a cold, killer smile as she gave a slow nod. "Damn straight."

"How? How do I even start to figure any of this out?"

"With the best damn tracker in the city, that's how. How on earth do you think I found you? I tracked you all the way to Balefire's and then to that weird teacher...and then to the edge of Never."

"The Ancient," I murmured.

"That's where he lives, right? All alone, tucked away from it all."

"Not all of it, no. I found someone spying on him, a mortal pretending to be a food source, but he was there listening to everything we said."

Her eyes widened. "Holy shit, not even the Ancients are safe now? That means whoever this is will stop at nothing to get what they want."

She took a step, turned and flopped down on the bed beside me. I gave a nod. "Nowhere is safe."

"So the only way out of this is to figure out who killed the mortal dude. Like I said before, that was a big ol' pile of blood on the bodyguard's floor..."

I shook my head. "Not Chuck."

"Really? Why not Chuck?"

"Because..." *He wouldn't do that. He wouldn't let me take the fall.*

"Only one way to find out, anyway." She rose from the bed and strode toward her bag. "Unless you got better things to do."

"Apart from sleep?" I mumbled.

A sharp bark of laughter came from the Wolf who was not my friend. "You'll have all the time in the world to sleep when you're dead."

She had a point.

I shoved up from the bed and stepped into my sneakers. "We gotta be careful, we can't be seen."

"Lucky for you, careful is my middle name," she muttered and hoisted her pack over her shoulders.

I glanced around the room, grabbed the hoodie and yanked it on. The clothes old and baggy, so far removed from anything I'd ever worn. This wasn't me, not my clothes. I lifted my hand skimmed through my damp hair.

But maybe that was perfect? Maybe that's exactly who I needed to be...not me, not Morwenna Livingstone. I glanced at Huntleigh and her dirty pack. "I'll carry your pack."

Her eyes widened, there was an instant shake of her head. "Nope, sorry. The pack stays with me."

There was a soft knock at the door. Shadows moved underneath the doorframe. Huntleigh was already reaching for her pack, sliding her hand inside the opening to pull out a small cross bow.

I stared at the weapon, and then her. With a shake of my head, I strode toward the door. "Easy, the door's been spelled. The entire Academy's has wards, no one's coming in here who wants to hurt me."

I turned the handle and yanked open the door and sure enough, there was a pile and a note once more. A cap, and a jacket sat on top of an old backpack. I reached down and grasped the note. *It's a boomerang. Meaning, I want the damn things back.*

I couldn't help but smile and shook my head. This was the one time I didn't mind someone eavesdropping. I grasped the things, finding lumps in the pack and stood from the doorway.

"What's that?"

"Something I'm going to need, I expect." I closed the door, yanked my cap on and made for the bed.

There was something inside the backpack, something that rattled, another something cold and hard. I pushed my hand into the opening and felt the hum of power. The vibration carried along my arm and to my body, standing my hair on end.

"What the Hell are those?" Huntleigh muttered as I dragged the steel thing free.

They were knuckles, brass knuckles. But not any type of knuckles, these were engraved with spells. An ache flared through my chest, like power called to power, and the faint remnant of Hekate blazed to life.

I put them on the bed and reached in once more. A small glass jar nestled in the palm of my hand, something rattled inside.

"Are those...*peppercorns?*" She stepped closer behind me.

There was a note taped to the side. *If these don't work, try the knuckles. Good luck, Desteny.*

"Whoever this Desteny is, she is one cool ass chick," Hunteight muttered.

She was, very cool, and very scary.

I stared into the bag and found a small zip lock pouch, so I pulled it out. Inside lay a round piece of glass. It came with a note.

Moon glass. Keep it on you at all times as it will come in handy for a boost.

I shoved the peppercorns and the brass knuckles back inside the pack and then rolled the jacket up tight and packed it in on top. The Moon glass I pushed into the pocket of my jeans.

With the cap on and pressing my hair down low, coupled with the hoodie meant no one would recognize me.

I wasn't a Livingstone. I wasn't anybody, and that's exactly what I needed it to be. I grabbed the pack as Huntleigh made for the window. "Um, how about we take the front door?"

She glanced at the open window and then gave a shrug. "Sure, we can do that."

I felt good leaving Blood Moon Academy, even if my thoughts were slow and my footsteps even slower. I had a plan, which was better than I had when I'd arrived.

I strode out of the room, hearing the thud of the door behind me and walked down the hall. A hum along my arms made my steps slow several doors down from mine. The feeling continued as I strode along the hallway.

I let instinct carry us back to the stairs, and somehow it didn't fail me. The place was quiet as we reached the stairs and made our way to the front door. Some part of me cringed with what we had to do.

I hated the idea of sneaking into Chuck's place, and I hated the thought of spying on him even less. Soft chants called out from somewhere behind me as I walked along the familiar hallway to the front door.

CHAPTER NINE

BLOOD ON THE FLOOR

"Looks quiet to me." Huntleigh scanned the dorms and other buildings.

I couldn't look away from the small cottage on the outskirts of Bestias Academy grounds. I swallowed the ache in the back of my throat. I didn't think I'd miss the stupid house and the stupid dorms. I didn't think I'd want anything more than to walk back through those doors, head to my room and slip into my boring life again.

It felt like an eternity since I'd been here. But it was only hours. Hours of running. Hours of being the victim. I settled my gaze on the empty driveway to the cottage; there was no more playing the victim now. "Let's go."

I shoved up to stand, took another glance along the quiet path, this time searching for Balefire's Hellhound guards, and then stepped out of the thick treeline.

"Keep your head down," Huntleigh growled beside me.

I lowered my gaze, grabbed the straps of my pack.

"And walk slow and normal." She strode ahead.

Walk slow and normal? I'm a damn Vampire, nothing about me is normal. I clenched my jaw and pushed on, my gaze fixed on the small, trimmed hedges along the side of the house.

It looked like Chuck wasn't here. I felt a stab of guilt, and a flicker of pain. Where was he right this minute? *With Ava,* the voice inside my head answered. *Where else would he be?*

I cut a glance to the dorms as a guard stepped around from the tree line further down and headed toward us. Huntleigh was already moving.

"Hahaha, and then you know what the Alpha said? He said *fang it.*" She threw her head back and laughed, before giving me a shove.

The act was perfect, driving me half a step forward so she could step around me, and stand on the other side. I tried not to look at him, tried to keep my head down. Tried not to feel the terror pushing in as the Hellhound called out. "Hey, stop right there."

Huntleigh gave a savage sigh and then stilled, swinging her gaze to the towering male. "What is it now? I was just literally stopped a second ago."

I didn't dare lift my head and meet his gaze as he snarled. "No students are supposed to be out here, didn't you read the notice?"

"Oh, I read the notice, but you try telling Mr. Gomez. He wants us out here looking for some damn berry."

"Gomez?" The Hellhound barked. "What class is that?"

"Rites and Rituals," she muttered with a shrug. "He said he doesn't care about any notice though. There's more students out here, in fact I think a heap went toward the Lodge."

There was a cold, calculated sneer hidden under the guise of innocence. She just lifted her gaze and stared at him.

"Goddamn teachers, pain in my fucking ass," he muttered and grabbed a two-way from his belt.

The stinging stench of burning plastic wafted to my nose as the Hellhound turned and stalked away. Tiny puffs of white smoke came from around his grip as he pressed the button and roared into the device. "Yellow, there's another group of students out here. They say there's more heading to the damn library."

There was a crackle and then a hiss from the radio as he walked away. He shook the damn thing as more white smoke came from around his fingers. Seemed like plastic and pissed off Hellhound didn't mix—who would've thought.

"Let's go," Huntleigh muttered, pushing me toward the cottage.

I hurried, head down like a good, normal Vampire. Nothing to see here, folks, just keep on walking. I stepped behind the hedge and slipped down the side of the house.

"I don't have a key," I whispered.

"That's okay, I don't have one either." Huntleigh yanked out a small leather pouch from her pack.

I stared at the bag. A cross-bow and a lock pick set, what else did she have in there? A sniff and a growl came from the other side of the rear door. I crouched as Huntleigh set to work on the lock and pressed my hand to the wood. "Jabba, it's me."

He gave a snarl and a tiny yelp. For a second I felt like I'd let this creature down too. He'd been my birthday gift from Dad. Something special to celebrate the massive milestone of turning one hundred, and even though Dad fucked up and bought me a badger instead of a fox, I'd fallen in love with him.

Only, to love something like Jabba wasn't enough, you

had to be there, care for him, you had to do more than just want for him.

"Okay," she said as the door clicked. "We're in."

I stood and watched her stow the leather pouch into her bag. She was unexpected, this Wolf, and that was putting it mildly. Long brown hair fell in tangles around her shoulders as she reached around her pack and then back to the door. "You ready to do this, Vampire?"

I gave a nod, steeled myself and stepped inside. I had no other choice, I had to find out if the blood on Chuck's floor was the Commissioner's, and if it wasn't his blood, then who's blood was it?

Jabba gave a snuff and lunged forward, beady black eyes shining bright as it curled its lips and bared sharp savage teeth.

"It's okay," I murmured and reached for him.

But to him I was a stranger, to him I was someone trespassing.

"Ugh, can't stand rodents," Huntleigh snapped and reached for her pack once more.

All I could envision was the weapon inside that bag. "*No!*" I roared. "He's fine, he's just scared."

I reached for him, desperation bursting inside me. "It's okay, Jabba. You know me. We're not gonna hurt you."

"Jeez, relax will ya. I was just getting a damn peanut bar for the gremlin," Huntleigh muttered and lifted a bar to her mouth. Sharp, pointed fangs tore the top of the wrapping before she broke a chunk free.

Honey glistened over the peanuts as she crouched down. "Here you go, little fella. You like honey, right?"

Jabba sniffed the air and gave a tiny growl. But it was half-hearted at best and his little shining eyes never moved from the treat in Huntleigh's hand.

"Go on, take it," she urged and stretched forward.

He was a flash of movement, nails tapping and scratching on the floorboards as he scurried forward, snatched the morsel from her hand and ran away.

"That's the way, killer. There's plenty more where that came from."

She folded the top of the packet and tucked it away in her pocket as she rose. "Right, let's see what we can find."

It seemed like I had her all wrong. I glanced to her open pack and swallowed a flare of guilt. She was here, willing to risk her own safety for me.

"Thank you," I started.

She held up a hand, waving me away. "Not interested in that. Not yet. You can thank me when this is all finished. *If* we both survive that is."

She crossed herself then, warding her words. I had no choice but to follow her into the cottage. If I thought I didn't really know her before, then right now I was way out of my depths.

"Always wondered what this place looked like on the inside."

The way she said it didn't sit right. "Always? You've only been at the Academy a month."

There was that shrug again as she knelt at the corner of the kitchen counter, right where the blood had been spilled across the floor. She pressed her fingers against the ground and then dropped lower.

Fingers widened, splayed as she braced her hands on the ground and inhaled. There was a wrinkling of her nose, before a low, warning growl came from her throat. Jabba scurried across the hallway and disappeared through a door.

"What is it?" I stepped closer.

She whipped her head up, the silver glint in her eyes

shining bright. "Nothing," she answered, but her voice was warped and strange. She pushed to her feet, and strode from the kitchen.

I followed her as she went into Chuck's bedroom.

"There's nothing here." I glanced around the room

Everything was perfect and neat. There wasn't even a wrinkle in the bedsheets. I leaned down and pressed my palm to the blanket.

"I wouldn't do that if I were you," she murmured glancing around the room.

My gaze narrowed. "Why?"

She straightened slowly and turned her head, meeting my gaze. "You really don't know, do you?"

I could only stand there and shake my head.

"Do you really know Chuck at all?" she murmured. "I mean the Vampire's been your bodyguard forever. Do you know what he was before he came to work for your father?"

I flinched. I didn't like this, not her words or her accusations.

She just shook her head. "Vampires? You really need to do a little background check before you hand over your best friend on a platter."

My breath caught. "Tell me."

She lifted her head, sniffed the air. "You know the saying...if I tell you...then I'm gonna have to..." Her voice trailed off.

"Kill me?" I answered for her.

She wasn't paying any attention to me, or the bombshell she just dropped. Instead, she strode toward the cupboard at the end of the hall and ran her fingers along the opening.

But she never touched the handle, only stared at the gap between the wall and the door.

"What are you doing?" I stepped closer, watching her fingers as she felt along the crevice, higher...higher...*higher*.

"Why don't you just—" I reached for the handle as she pressed against the jam.

There was a tiny click, before terrifying, two inch, sharpened spikes shot out from the steel handle.

"That's why," she snarled, cut me a glare and then leaned down. "Niiicceee, laced with poison too. Heartweed if I smell correctly. Kill a human in a second flat. Make a damn Immortal sick enough that they'd see visions of their maker. Still think your Vamp is Mr. Sweet and Innocent?" she muttered as she drew a blade from her pocket and wedged the tip between the frame.

I stared at those wicked spines, envisioning Ava's smiling face as laughed and joked. *Come on Chucky, I want to dress you today...* She'd reach for the handle. She'd impale her hand...and she'd die.

That's what'd happen, my best friend would die because someone set a trap. The door opened with a *click* and swung free, and curled with bare knees to a bare chest was a dead guy.

"I'll take door number two, Nigel," Huntleigh murmured and folded the blade against her hip.

She squatted, not yet reaching out. I knew more than to instruct her now...I now knew to wait.

She looked at him for a long time, leaning close to sniff the air. He was thick and muscled.

"Grazes on his knuckles," she murmured and jerked her head toward his hands. One lay flat on the floor at his side. I couldn't see where the other one was. I envisioned the dead guy with one less arm, the other flapping uselessly as he wailed and thrashed.

"Ewww."

"What?" Huntleigh jerked her gaze to mine.

I just shook my head. "Nothing, sorry."

"Don't say sorry to me," she muttered and leaned forward. "I'm not the one holed up in your bodyguard's closet drained entirely of blood." She reached for his face, gripping his jaw, turning his head, and then searched what she could of his naked body without moving him an inch.

But as she shifted his arm, I saw something. A blue light under his skin...the same kind of blue light I'd seen before. "Stop."

Huntleigh stilled, jerked her head up. "What now?"

"His hand, that light."

She shot me a glare. "What damn light."

I was loath to touch him. Visions of dead guys hands on my boob re-emerged, still I knelt, swallowed hard and reached out. Three dots were revealed against his wrist. "See this." I pressed my fingers to his flesh. "I've seen that recently."

It was my turn to know something she didn't. "The mortal spying on me when I spoke to the Ancient had the same exact mark."

Her brows narrowed, a line creased down the middle of her forehead. "Dead guy's a spy," she murmured. "That makes a whole lot of sense."

I exhaled and closed my eyes. It wasn't Chuck. It wasn't Chuck who killed the Commissioner. It wasn't Chuck who set me up. I slumped forward, reached out to touch the doorframe and sat back, my spine hitting the bed. "Thank you, Lucifer." I murmured. "Thank you."

"I don't know why you're so damn relieved. You still don't know who killed the commissioner."

"But at least I know who it wasn't," I answered and that felt so much better than knowing who did.

I understood what I was capable of now, and it wasn't power and strength.

It was knowing what kind of knowledge I could live with...and what knowledge I couldn't.

"You think it's Judas?" she murmured.

Judas? I glanced at her. There was a cringe like the mere whisper of a *yes* would be felt as a slap. "No, I don't. He was with me the entire time, same as Nero. We were fighting Lions for Hell's sake. There was no way they could leave, race all the way to where the Commissioner lived, kill him and then get back in time."

"Then who could it be?" she muttered.

I grew colder. Colder than I'd ever felt before as a face filled my mind.

A flare of agony cut through my chest. My shoulders curled with the pain.

A killing blow.

"I..." His smile, his laugh... His absence. The past seemed to open up and swallow me whole. "If I asked you to let me search on my own, would you?"

She whipped her gaze toward me. "Do you really want me to let you?"

"Yes...I think I do for this one." I shoved my hand against the floor and pushed to stand. "I think I have to...even if I don't want to know."

"It's your funeral," she murmured. "If you need me, I'll be around."

I just gave a nod and turned away from her. I couldn't look at the bed now, couldn't look at the walls or the floors. I couldn't look at anything, my world was turned within.

Jabba chuffed and growled from the end of the hallway. But I couldn't give him the love I wanted to. I just left him behind.

I made my way to the open rear door and slipped through. I needed to get back to the trees, and the cold wind. I needed to get back to that aching loneliness.

That bitter despair.

Some part of me wished it had been Chuck.

Then maybe it wouldn't hurt as bad.

CHAPTER TEN

BRUISED KNUCKLES. SAVAGE BEAST

Night came while I waited. It slipped in, taking me by surprise while I sat huddled against the base of a tree. I stared toward the ground. I stared toward my hand. Still I couldn't see them. I didn't want to be here now. I didn't want to be sitting outside the dorm rooms waiting for strangers. I didn't want to face them, to demand from them. I didn't want to try to understand.

Lights blinked on in the room overhead. I sucked in a hard breath and then lifted my gaze.

Not him...

Not him...

Please not him...

The light flicked off again. I braced my hand against the dirt and shoved to stand. True to her word, Huntleigh was long gone, leaving barely a whisper behind. A growl echoed from somewhere inside the dorm, followed by another, and then another. They were angry, turning on each other.

Minutes later the door opened and a dark silhouette stepped out. Blond hair shimmered in the lights before he was gone, head down, shoulders hunched with hands shoved into the pockets of his dark hoodie.

My heart gave a tremble and then a thud as I turned and followed. I hated this, this awful poisonous feeling—this *treachery*. He moved fast, long strides cutting across the grassed area before in a slow bound he pushed into a run.

Ground-eating strides swept through the trees. I shoved forward, breaking into a run further up from him. If he turned his head, he'd see me bounding between the trees. But he never did. Lost in his own thoughts, Bond left the Academy grounds behind and raced toward the city.

I swept my hand in front of me, shoving aside branches and leaves as I tried to keep up. He was graceful, barely snapping a twig, heavy thudding strides timed so perfectly they were like the heartbeat of the earth.

I fumbled like an idiot, short, sharp strides, follow by bounding ones like a damn gazelle. My thighs were on fire by the time we left the forest behind and stepped out into the opening with the city lights blinking in front of us. I sucked in hard breaths and slowed down, letting him get a little ahead before I followed. Still he never paid me any mind, seemingly lost in his thoughts.

I followed, waiting for him to get further along the darkened street before I slipped from car to car with my cap and my hoodie pulled low. The disguise was perfect. I wasn't me in these clothes. All the horror seemed to belong to someone else, another Vampire, another woman. But I was the one to save her...even if all I could do was save her heart.

Bond glanced both ways before he slipped into an alley. My heart trembled with the motion as I stepped out from behind a minivan and followed. I was on the hunt, but this time my prey was the Wolf I cared for.

I turned into the alley, blinked into the darkness as my

eyes adjusted and then listened for his footsteps as they softly rang out. A car alarm sounded somewhere behind me. Gunshots followed, screams carried after that. I flinched and looked over my shoulder.

I didn't like this side of the city. It was a place of thugs and murdered, of bullies and beasts. I'd been here once with Dad and Chuck, and swore to myself I'd never step foot here again. But here I was, not only following someone down a darkened alley unprotected, I was pretending to be one of them.

Bond turned again, stepping down an even darker narrow side street. No cars could get down this, only those on foot. A can rattled as it rolled along the ground. Dumpsters reeked, spilling out torn bags of waste.

The scent of old blood carried on the wind to fill my nose. My stomach clenched as I waited, hovering at the entrance to the narrow lane, and glanced around the corner to where Bond stopped halfway along the passage.

He stared at a wall, hands shoved deep into his pockets, until the squeal of metal hinges rang out. Deep mumbled growls barely reached my ears before Bond stepped through the door.

Faint screams and howls drifted into the passageway until the door closed with a *bang*, leaving silence behind. I waited, gathering all the courage I could find and followed.

My steps rang out far too loud as I made my way to where he disappeared. I could hear them...whoever they were. Shouts and screams filled the belly of this building, like it was a ravenous beast.

I reached out and pressed my hand against the cold bricks and felt the power race through me. Flashes of darkness and death. Terrible flashes. Haunting flashes. I wrenched my hand free, slamming fingers to my chest, and inside that hollow ache the remnant of the Diamonds' power flickered to life.

It was a warning, a terrifying warning...*leave this place* the power whispered...*run.*

I glanced to the faint outline of the door and swallowed that surge of need. I couldn't, not until I knew if Bond had murdered the Commissioner.

I stepped up to the door and reached out. For a second my knuckles hovered an inch from the steel. I didn't want to touch it, didn't want to feel that sickening fear and hunger. I closed my eyes and swayed for a second before perfect green eyes filled my mind.

I could still see his cheeky smile, still feel the heat of his body on mine, still feel the desire that blazed between us, and it was that love I held onto as I opened my eyes, stepped forward and knocked.

The door was yanked open before I registered and the hateful sneer of a Wolf filled my view.

"What?" the battle scarred Beta snarled.

Eyes drifted over me, lingered at my chest.

"I want in," I murmured.

"So do I honey, I'll let you in for a blow job, how about that?" He took a step outside into the passage. "What's a pretty little thing like you doing here, you know what kind of men walk down this alley?"

He reached for my face and I recoiled. "I have a fair idea."

He smiled then, lips pulling back from disgusting blackened teeth.

"How about this," I murmured and took a step backwards. He stepped when I did, thinking he was the predator, and little ol' weak me, was the prey.

"Yeah?" he murmured and swiped the back of his hand

across his nose. "Whatcha gonna do for me, precious?"

I turned inwards, hurtling down into that dark depth of power that lingered inside me and said, "How about I let you live?"

It was my turn to step forward, my turn to be what he wasn't...I reached out with my hand and unleashed that hunger from inside. His eyes widened with the flare of power. But it wasn't quite enough. Just a trickle from the cavern inside me.

His eyes widened as a moan tore from his lips. Panic rose inside me as he stumbled backwards. I lunged, fists raised before I swung and drove all my strength through the arc, hitting him in the jaw.

The punch was lucky. His head snapped backwards, knees buckled before he fell in slow motion. I scurried forward, sneakers slapping on the ground and caught the shifter under the arms. "Easy," I murmured, glancing toward the doorway, to where the shouts and screams came from.

I didn't know what was in there, but I was willing to bet if I carried the Wolf inside someone would notice. I scanned the alley, finding a dumpster full to overflowing further down.

His boots scraped along the ground as I stumbled backwards, heaving him toward the stench. "Just have a nice little nap," I murmured and winced. There wasn't much space between the dumpster and the wall. I eased him to the ground and then hurried to the corner, gripped the side and heaved.

Metal scraped before the roller gave way. All I needed was a little space, just enough to cover him. Muscles strained as I yanked and then straightened.

Still his legs stuck out. I glanced along the alley and

resigned myself to this fate. "Can't believe I'm doing this," I muttered, and strode toward his feet.

I bent, grabbed his boots and lifted, hauling his limbs into the air and then pushed.

Tendons pulled until they stopped. But I shoved, and braced his boots against the side of the dumpster and then stepped back.

He was squashed, ass on the ground, his feet higher than his head. "Try explaining that to yourself when you wake up."

The roar of a crowd slipped through the open door. I left the meathead behind, hoping he'd not walk properly for at least a week and made for the open door. Bond was all I cared about, that and getting the Hell out of this place alive.

My legs shook as I stepped inside and closed the door behind me. It was a narrow passageway, leading where, I didn't know, but I followed the screams and the shouts. The paint was worn on the concrete floor, the walls dirty and marred. Old blood smeared like a thumbprint at shoulder height. I kept on walking, pushing through a half open door to step out onto a landing and froze.

Carnage filled my view, blood and terror mingling with wide-eyed excitement and adrenaline. Men, women...mortals and immortals all gathered around the makeshift ring screaming...*Kill him! Kill him, now! Hurt him! I said, hurt him!*

I trembled with the sound, reaching up to slap my hands over my ears as my gaze slipped to the two men inside the barrier. Two shifters flanked each other, bloodied and broken. Silver eyes glinted from the Wolf as he moved, the other had an arm which had shifted to a wing, the tip trailing on the ground as he stumbled.

An Eagle.

He was Flighter, a special breed of Immortal, man and bird combined. He'd tried to escape this place, half shifting as he was attacked. He didn't get far.

Kill him!

Even with my hands over my ears, I still flinched. My heart crawled through my chest and into my mouth. Why in the hell was Bond here? I lowered my hands, slowly stepped forward and gripped the railing. I walked down the steel industrial staircase watching as the Wolf inside the ring threw his head back and howled.

It was a howl of torment.

A howl of pain.

It was a howl of hate, and in an instant it stopped. I turned away as he moved behind the wall of beasts. The sickening *snap* of bone sent a deafening cheer through the crowd.

They got what they'd come for.

Acid spilled into my mouth. I stumbled forward, swallowing that bitter taste.

My soul seemed to slip further from the surface, falling far below. I was past the point of no return here, even if I left with Bond by my side, I'd hear this terror for the rest of my undead life.

I hit the ground as a woman shoved past. But she never paid me any attention, no one did. My eyes shimmered, cheeks flushed. This cesspit of foulness was full of those who were blood-drugged and high. Still I searched every face, every set of eyes, hoping to see that glint of perfect green.

"Now, the fight you've been waiting for!" someone screamed. "He's *undefeated,* an absolute animal, and he's up against an Alpha twice his size! Give it up for Bond the Brutal!"

My steps froze, senses seemed to slip away from me as movement came from the corner of my eye.

No.

No. No. No.

Bond strode toward that pit of death, head down, bare from the waist up with a blood stained pair of shorts hanging from his waist. He stared at the ground as the crowd parted in front of him. I wanted to scream his name, to rush forward and steal him away. But I couldn't move, frozen by fear....

He lifted his gaze and then turned to glance over his shoulder. I followed the look to the large windows of an office. A man stood behind the glass, looking out. He was big, hulking shoulders, thick neck. Something passed between them before Bond turned back.

The crowd screamed once more, some waving fists full of money in the air and screaming his name. I'd seen money. I'd seen greed, and I'd seen power. But I'd never seen this.

This was lunacy.

I didn't want to watch, didn't want to see what was left of the man I'd fallen in love with. "Bond!" I screamed and took a step forward. But my desperation was quickly swallowed by the roar of the crowd.

I turned my head as movement came toward me. I looked up...and up, past the thick shoulders to cold, killer eyes. Scars marred the Alpha's face. Deep grooves, jagged silver lines...*a beast.* That's what he looked like. A beast.

He looked right through me as he walked past, silver glint shining bright for a second before he turned away and was swallowed by the crowd.

He's going to kill Bond.

The words filled me, and there was no denying their truth.

He was going to kill the man I loved. I started forward as I lost sight of him in the crowd. Screams and howls of chilling laughter rang loud in my ears. But all I could hear was the heavy *thud...thud...thud...*of my bloodless heart.

"*Fight!*" someone screamed.

I jerked my head toward the sound as a sickening male roar came from inside, and was followed by a brutal blow. I shoved my fist into my belly and stumbled backwards, pressing my spine against the cold concrete wall.

It was to keep the sound in, no doubt, to keep the cheers and snapping of bone from leaking into the city streets. Did they know? Did the people of Tricks City know the barbarity of what went on here? Did they laugh and cheer above this Hell, just like they did in the pit?

Fists on flesh rang out. I wanted to close my eyes as I caught Bond stumble before the crowd moved and he was lost. I wanted to close my ears to the sounds of blows as they sounded over and over and over again.

I don't know how long I stood there.

I don't know how long the fight went on for.

Roars of madness coupled with fists of money.

Bond screamed and I screamed too. I screamed for him. I screamed for me. I screamed because there wasn't a damn thing I could do to save him. He was in Hell, all alone.

Until there was silence.

The crowd was still, wide eyed, staring at the middle of the ring. *He's dead. Bond is dead.*

My heart lunged as I stumbled forward, movement came from the stairs on my right. The shifter from the ring now standing at the door shook his head, gripped the railing and stumbled forward, movements jerking, the wince of pain bright in his eyes.

But I didn't care about him. I didn't care about anyone but Bond.

"Move." I shoved a mortal. He was craning his head to get a better view.

They wanted to see more of the blood. They wanted to see more of the carnage. I stepped on something hard and then it was soft. I looked down to see a long, brown wing feather. The tip was painted red. I swallowed the sting of acid in the back of my throat and shoved forward, past a wolf who screamed in my ear and a woman who waved two fists in the air and roared "Kill him! *Kill HIM!*"

No. No this can't be...no this...can't...be. I pushed and shoved, driving my hands through the gaps and barged people out of the way. They were like zombies, but instead of brains, these creatures fed on death.

Then I was through, standing in the front line, staring down at the broken man on the ground. I sucked in heavy breaths. Bond was kneeling, bloodied, beaten. His eye was swollen and split. There was blood in his ear that dripped down his neck.

There was death in his eyes, death so close to the surface. His hands wrapped around the old Alpha's neck. There was no fight left in the older Wolf. His arm hung twisted and broken at his side, bone poked through the skin. The other arm was bloodied and gnawed; the same blood that coated Bond's lips.

One twist of his grip was all it'd take. One twist and he'd give them what they paid for...*what they screamed for.*

He lifted his head once more. I knew what he was staring at...the man behind the glass...the man in charge of it all.

"You want him dead?" Bond growled and then dropped the broken Alpha. "Kill him your goddamn self."

The crowed screamed and raged. But Bond was beyond caring. He was beyond reach.

He shoved upwards, stumbled until he caught his footing and then pushed through the crowd. He was gone in a roar of pissed off people, leaving a broken Alpha behind.

Someone stepped in, a male, big, savage. I knew he was different...and I knew what he was there to do. I turned away as the *crunch* of bone rang out. But the crowd was already turning. They wanted their shattered bones and their pound of flesh, but they'd wanted Bond to give it to them.

I followed him, through the hateful stares and spitting snarls, to the doorway and then along the hall. Still he never turned his head, never heard my steps haunting him, just as they'd done since the Academy grounds.

He turned and pushed through a doorway. There was blood on the paint, blood on the door frame...blood on his hands.

The echo of my footsteps was the only sound I was alive. Inside I felt dead and barren. I was thankful it wasn't him on that ground, that is wasn't him being carted away to never be seen again.

The squeal of a locker tore through the dressing room. I rounded the end of the long straight rows until he came into view. He didn't lift his head, he didn't see me...not at first.

"Bond," I whispered.

He went still, so still I thought he didn't hear me speak.

Until he wrenched his head upwards, and slowly turned to meet my gaze. "Mor?"

Surprise raged, followed by panic as he glanced at the empty shower stalls and the dressing room behind me.

"What are you doing, Bond? Tell me right now...what in Hell's name are you doing?"

CHAPTER ELEVEN

UNRAVELING TRUTHS

"Tell me why, Bond?" Images of him in the ring bounced around in my head. I dug and dug for clues but deep in my gut I knew the truth. My instincts, that I had ignored earlier, ripped through me, and I couldn't admit to myself that Bond might have killed the Commissioner.

He didn't respond but turned from me, staring blankly toward the line of empty shower stalls. The moment felt so stretched, I sunk beneath the darkness of my thoughts.

I reached out for him, grasped for his arm but he pulled away from me. "Go away, Mor. Leave this place. It's not for someone like you."

There was something behind those angry words, something painful. I watched him, his curled posture, the fisted hands.

Fire raged inside me to have him push me aside, to know he'd been holding onto this secret alone for so long.

"You think I'm weak? You think I can't handle a pit of monsters? Because that's all you were out there. A monster," I cried out, fury threading behind my voice.

He jerked around to face me, and I saw it.... The pain in his eyes like it had been there a lifetime, trapped and drowning him. But I saw so much more. Love. How much he cared.

His arms shook by his side, and my heart turned jagged. He stood before me, naked from the waist up, his chest glistening with sweat, bloody and bruised from the fight, muscles flexing, but he was vulnerable. Still, he held back the truth, concealed it with layers of the wall he'd built to hide behind.

"Please, Bond, let me in because it's killing me to see you like this."

His brow furrowed and he lowered his head, shadows concealing his expression as he shook his head. If he had any tears left, he'd be crying.

"I read somewhere that only warriors choose their battles. This is my fight, so let me do what I need," he growled. Once again, he turned from me, leaving me behind.

"This isn't just your fight." I strode forward, grabbed his wrist, and swung him around. "Tell me why? Why are you doing this?"

He shuddered and quaked under my touch, and when he met my gaze, the hurt creased the corners of his eyes. "Because someone perfect like you shouldn't be tainted by a place like this. Because you're right. There are monsters... and I'm the worst one."

"That's not true." I squeezed his arm.

"I can't offer you the brightness you deserve, Mor, can't you see that? I've done things... things that I hate. Every night I go to sleep and see myself lowered in my grave. I wake up with a scream on my throat. I'm too far gone and you're better off without me." He ripped his hand from mine.

Scared.

He looked so close to breaking... on the edge, needing any excuse to fall. I chased after him, refusing to let go.

His hand curled around my fingers softly, and the first threads of hope appeared like a tiny flicker of light in his eyes. But he shook his head, chasing away the promise, and he grumbled under his breath. "I already hurt you so much."

This time when he tried to rip free, I held on like a lifeline, digging fingers into flesh, needing him to understand that we stuck together through thick and thin.

"You don't even know the things I've done." The gravel in his voice brought out so much hatred in his words, and he refused to look me in the eyes.

"Then tell me," I pleaded.

But he fell silent again, lost in his own world.

"If you think you have nothing left to lose," I began. "Then you have no reason not to trust in me."

His head hung low, shoulders curled, when the door to the change room swung open.

Bond's head jerked up and his posture straightened.

I spun around, my gaze skimming over the huge man who entered the room.

He stood tall, unshaven, shaggy hair framing his large, round head. Shoulders so wide, he could carry the world on them. He heaved each breath, heavy and short, and his eyes were the deepest brown... I inhaled the air, his barnyard and fur smell finding me and I gasped.

Bear shifter.

With three healed claw marks across his nose and

cheek, it looked like he didn't back down from any fight. Bears were notoriously dangerous and unpredictable. Dressed in navy slacks and a matching windbreaker, zipped up, he reminded me of a pimp. His attention soared to Bond.

Their exchange was primal... challenging, and neither backed down.

"What is she doing here? Vamps are fucking corpses, or are you into that kinky shit." He grunted like a boar. "I'll take her off your hands as payment."

Before I could respond, Bond stepped in front of me, his hand on my arm, pushing me out of sight.

All I could feel was the tension in the air, everything else faded away.

Bond would protect me. He'd fight to the end. And I'd have his back.

My insides turned cold and I glanced around the room for another way out, but it was useless. No other exit or windows.

"She has nothing to do with this," Bond snarled.

Footsteps hit the concrete, and I peered out from behind Bond to the giant who looked ready to rip off our heads. "Next time they say to kill, you do it like the dog that you are," he barked in Bond's face.

The words cut through my mind, and I couldn't believe my ears.

They.

Kill.

Who the fuck was behind this?

They'd demanded Bond kill someone in the ring. But they didn't... and if he was responsible for the Commissioner's death, it might mean someone forced him? So, what did they have over him?

He didn't respond to the Bear, but stood his ground, solid, chin lifted. My Wolf was a fighter and damn brave. There was so much to admire about him, and I adored his protectiveness, his determination. It did something to me... to have someone lay their life down for me brought out my primal instinct. I adored Bond and I was prepared to fight by this side.

"Next time," the bear growled and shoved a hand into Bond's chest, but he held his ground, didn't stumble backward.

"When they say to kill, *you kill*," he roared, spittle flying over Bond. "Otherwise next time, they're coming after *you*. And they'll take your pretty girlfriend here too."

My hands shook as the bear spun and marched out of the room, slamming the door shut behind him.

Bond quietly turned. He reached a hand toward me and with a thumb wiped away the first tear to fall. Defeat washed over his expression, and I could tell he knew there was no backing out now. Whatever was happening would drag him deeper until he drowned.

"I lied before," he admitted. "Judas gave me that photo in the room under the church." He walked to a nearby locker and opened it before digging his hand inside.

His Academy clothes were neatly folded, packed away like he lived two lives... the fighter and the student, the complete opposite of one another—a man and a monster. Somehow, he'd been forced into this life, and it maddened me to see him suffering so much.

From inside the locker, he pulled out a scrunched up photo and straightened it in his hands. I looked down at the image, at the girl with sandy hair who smiled, her green eyes wide and innocent.

Bond's sister.

"It's my fault. I was supposed to watch out for Evie. I was supposed to be her big brother. But that day... that day she just nagged and nagged and nagged, begging me to let her go hunting for wildberries. I finally gave in and said yes, just to shut her up. Just so I could be by myself." His breaths grew sharp and raspy, but unlike before he held my gaze. No turning away or pushing me. "They took her..." he snarled. "And now I fight for them to get her back."

Nausea welled unrestrained in my stomach. My head swam with pain. I should've figured this out earlier. If I had, then maybe....

Darkness folded around me. *They* used Bond's sister as leverage to control him. They tormented him...ripped apart his innocence. To them he was nothing more than a killer—nothing more than a *beast*.

I shook my head as his ache filled me. He turned to look at me with those same perfect green eyes, the same Bond I loved, right here, desperate for me to make him whole once again. "Who are they?" I snarled.

He shrugged. "The Commissioner took my sister, and now his pack of mongrels force me to pay a debt to get Evie back." He cast his gaze upward, defeated, shattered.

I dragged him closer, and his arms instinctively looped around me, pressing us together. His breaths were racing, and he clung to me, his stiffness easing as he accepted he couldn't do this on his own.

Still unsure if Bond killed the Commissioner, I couldn't ask him now... not when he'd been so open with me, not when he was hurting so much. Though I suspected the pack of mongrels who once reported to the Commissioner might have a new boss now, but I had no idea who.

"We'll find her." I leaned close to Bond, running my

hands along his biceps and then his shoulders. "I promise you on all that I am, we'll find her."

"How?" he whispered. "How when I can't even find her myself?"

By tearing them apart, that dark voice whispered inside me...*one...by...one.*

CHAPTER TWELVE

ONE STRIKE IS ALL IT TAKES

Doubt darkened his eyes to lush green grass. He shook his head and turned away. His voice husky, choked with emotion. "I just keep thinking to myself one more fight, one more time and they'll give her to me. One more...but it's always one more, isn't it?" He shoved the door to his locker closed with a *bang*. "One more dead Alpha, one more chance to put me in the grave. They don't care, they'll *never* care. As long as they get their money..." He lifted his gaze to stare at the lockers. "As long as they get their crowd."

"Then we don't give them the crowd." I strode forward. "We don't give them anything. We're not the ones powerless here. You might think we are, you might feel like we are. But we're not. They have more to lose than we'll ever have. All we have to do is turn this around, let them be the ones running scared for once...let *them* be the ones looking over *their* shoulder."

He limped when he walked. But he was strong, strong enough to be Alpha if he wanted. But that meant going up against Judas, and that just wasn't him. The Wolf in him healed his body, red marks darkened until I could almost draw the outline of a fist against his ribs. And then the bruised flesh turned yellow, already closing off the blood cells, and repairing the damage.

But no matter how strong he was, his immortal self couldn't heal his heart.

That was my job.

I stepped closer, catching his flinch as I lifted my hand. "Let me take care of you. Let me heal you."

He was Bond, my lover...*my friend.* "You don't want to touch me."

"I think you should let me be the judge of that."

There was a shake of his head. "I'm not good, Mor. I'm not kind, I'm not gentle. I'm not whole."

I stepped closer, sliding my hand down his arm to cup his hand. These hands had broken, but they also healed. I stepped closer, until my body pressed against his. I could feel the jump of his pulse. "You feel whole to me."

I couldn't save him from this Hell he found himself in. But I could stand here and shine a torch in the darkness. I could wait, guide him back. He needed me now, more than anyone had ever needed me before.

A battle of the flesh was one thing, but a battle of the soul was another thing entirely.

Give yourself, that voice whispered inside. *Give yourself to him now.*

I thought of the others, of the tortured look on Judas's face when Bond walked away. He'd not deny him this, not Bond, not when he lay in broken pieces. Judas would want me to go to him, to bring his Wolf back from the brink of destruction.

I'd do that for him. I'd do that for us.

I slid my hand around the back of his neck and whispered. "I am yours, and you are mine. I'd travel through eternity to save you."

Green eyes sparkled with the shine of silver. His beast was so close to the surface now. I could see the savageness, the hunger, see his lips curled from his teeth—see how scared he really was.

I lowered my head, kissing his arm, and then his shoulder, fully aware how vulnerable I was now. One bite at the back of my neck was all it'd take. He dropped his arms, hard breath blowing strands of my hair. I lifted my head, meeting his gaze, letting him see what I was prepared to give him.

I was prepared to give it all.

"Every touch," I whispered, my hand dancing along his arm. "Every kiss, every moan, every shudder."

His eyes widened, lips parted. His breath was mine to capture. I leaned closer, and then closed my eyes.

The warm brush of his lips was soft and tender. He barely moved, just opening his mouth a little wider, letting me in. His hand dropped to my waist, fingers trembling. In all the brutal, terrifying battles he'd fought and won, this was the one that made him tremble with fear.

This one made him quake.

Hands grew bolder, gripping my hips, pulling me hard against him. And in a torrent of need he broke against me, hands gripped my waist, lifting my body from the floor like I weighed nothing. He stumbled on, guiding me along the rows of lockers, kissing me with a ferocity I'd never felt before.

Cold steel at my back, hard body at my front, driving my thighs wider. I locked my feet around his hips and held on.

His hands trembled as he reached for the front of my hoodie, yanking it upwards, before fumbling with the button of my jeans. My breath caught as fingers delved, sliding under my panties to the sensitive flesh underneath.

He pushed against me, driving my spine against the locker and lowered his head. "I'm sorry," his voice was a growl of need. "I'm so sorry."

I held on, fingers gouging his shoulder as I threw my head backwards. Probing fingers slipped deeper, all the way inside. I rocked my hips against him, driving him deeper, wanting him all the way in. "Harder." Breathless whispers slipped free. "I want you harder."

He slipped and slid, thrusting his hips with the rhythm. I remembered the outline of him, remember the feel, remembered the thickness. "I want you, Bond. I want all of you."

My fingers slipped, falling to the heat between us, through the thin fabric of his shorts I could feel it all. He was hard and ready, and trembling. He lowered my feet to the ground, long enough to shove my jeans down. I kicked off my sneakers, letting them drop with a *thud.* Cool air licked between my thighs as Bond shoved my panties down.

His gaze followed the drag of his fingers as he ran the length of my slit. "Hell, you're beautiful." He met my gaze. "So fucking beautiful."

One shove of his boxers and he stood bare in front of me. Hard muscles of his stomach flexed and rolled, tightening to a deep V. I was drawn to the glistening thick thatch of dark hair, and the pulsing vein that ran the length of his cock.

"You okay with this." He slid his finger along my core, finding the slick.

I was more than ready, more than okay, more than anything. But words failed me, leaving me to meet his gaze and give a slow, small nod. In the wake of fumbling desperation, we found an ebb, slow, panting breaths. Our gazes locked.

He moved forward, leaving the desperate ache between my thighs behind to trail my own desire along my skin and lifted my leg.

Warmth met my core, probing, seeking. His skin almost fevered. But there was no illness in his eyes, no touch of anything other than unrelenting love. The tip of his cock pressed against me, finding the groove as I tilted my hips.

He pushed inside, just enough for me to catch my breath. He was too big, too hard, too everything. With a slow rock of my hips he pulled free, leaving me trembling until he tried again. His other hand went to my thigh, lifting me higher, bracing my back against the lockers.

Splayed wide against him, he pushed in until I closed my eyes and groaned. Panic flared for a second. This was a hunt I was unprepared for, a hunt I couldn't escape and as he rocked his hips, pushing all the way inside, I knew there was no turning back now—there never really had been.

I was his, just as he was mine. I drove my nails against his flesh and opened my eyes as he gave one brutal thrust, slamming me against the lockers. The steel shuddered, the *boom* deafening in my ears as he slid his hand along my spine.

There was only that hunger now, only that need...*deeper...harder*. He lowered me to the ground. Brutal thrusts drove my body along the cold icy floor of the locker room. But his grip on my hips pulled me back.

I reached for him, driving my feet harder around him as he curled his spine. That hunger was savage inside me, hunting...hunting...*hunting*. Fangs grew long, nicking the tender flesh inside my lips as hunger roared through my body.

"I love you." He lowered his head, curled his spine, until I became his anchor to this world. "I...*love...you.*"

Hope blazed silver and ravenous as I parted my mouth and raised my head. "I love you too." And with a roar of dark, predator power flooding my veins I wrenched him against me and bit.

Warmth filled my mouth as my body twitched, thrumming against him. Bond cried out against me. But I was a beast...a beautiful, undeniable beast. He jerked against me, driving his hips forward in one unforgiving thrust and then stilled.

My tongue skimmed the flesh of his neck. Fangs embedded in the vein. I swallowed as that heady rush swept through me and then gently pulled away.

Two puncture wounds over his vein healed quickly in a preservation of life, and the realization of what I'd just done swept over me in a rush.

I bit him.

I bit him like a Vampire, and drank from his vein.

What had I done? I reached for my throat waiting for the fire and the pain. But none came.

"What's wrong?" Bond shoved forward.

"Your blood. It's poison."

"Where on earth did you hear that?"

And I remembered my father's words. And then the blood in the church. "The Blood I drank. The one from the church."

"That was no wolf's blood, Mor. I don't know what it was. But it wasn't a Wolf's."

Power hummed through me, sliding down the back of my throat to well in my belly. I could taste his Wolf, taste the grass under my feet and the rush in my veins. I could feel everything he felt, the horror of what he'd done...the betrayal of his own kind.

I felt him like I'd never felt anyone before. What I had before was a glimpse standing on the outside looking in. But this. This was different. *This was more.* Like the remnant of dark power in my chest, his blood carried me to places without moving an inch.

"Are you...are you okay?" he whispered.

I flinched at the sound of his voice and came crashing back down. The wounds in his neck were only tiny pin pricks of red fading from view. He still cradled me, was still inside me. Soft, yielding, there was fear in his eyes, real fear I saw now...fear for me.

He was the one who'd been bitten. He was the one who'd felt the stab of pain, and yet in this moment *I* was the one he cared about. "I'm sorry," I whispered. "I don't know what came over me. I... I've never done that before."

Hope gave way to surprise. There was a slow sheepish hint of a smile as he whispered, "Then I'm glad I'm the first one."

"You don't mean that." I let my hand fall away, as the true realisation hit home. "I hurt you."

"Hurt me?" His brow furrowed. "You gave yourself to me. You gave me everything, without hesitation. That was the most thrilling experience of my life."

I couldn't think, couldn't feel, couldn't see anything but the humbling look of gratitude in his gaze.

"Has no one told you that Vampire's do that when they fall in love?" he murmured, concern flaring bright.

"No," I answered. "No, they never have. And you knew that before we..."

"I'd hoped you felt the same way as I do. I prayed for it even. I guess now I know. I love you, Morwenna Livingstone, the fact you swallowed my blood means you love me too."

All this time I thought I was different from the others of my kind.

All this time I felt half-fulfilled, it was all because of this.

I hadn't met my true mate.

I hadn't fallen in love.

CHAPTER THIRTEEN

BLOOD AND GOLD

Darkness moved into his eyes, like a thunderstorm, his expression changing from one of love to uncertainty. "We shouldn't have done this."

He pulled away, leaving me exposed and naked. I closed my thighs feeling the trickle of warmth slip free.

"No, stupid...*stupid,*" he snarled, and looked down at me like I was a stranger and backed away. "This was a mistake. A stupid fucking mistake."

"Where are you going?" I shoved up from the floor and reached for my panties. "What was a mistake? You mean me...you mean *this?*"

"We shouldn't be doing this." He snatched his boxers from the ground and stepped into them.

"Stop." Agony ripped through me and the hum in my body grew cold. I followed him, slipping my panties on and then followed with my jeans.

"I don't have anything left to give you." He stilled at his open locker, and yanked his jeans free. Hard muscles along his back rippling as he moved.

"What are you talking about?"

"You deserve better than me, better than this. I told you before, I'm not good. I'm broken Mor. I've got more blood on my hands than you can ever handle."

"You think *you* have blood on your hands?" I snarled and strode forward.

Anger tainted the perfection of our love. Still he wasn't listening, jerking his shirt over his head and down. "Bond, stop this madness. Let me understand."

"*Understand?*" he barked. "You can't begin to understand. You think I kill in the ring? You think that's the worst I've ever done?"

"Then *tell me.*" My fangs skimmed the tender skin of my lips.

I wanted to puncture. I wanted to bite.

"No." He shook his head and shoved his feet into his boots.

I lunged forward grasping his arm. *"Tell me!"*

He stilled, breaths heaving his shoulder before he turned to face me. "You really want to know? *You think you'll understand me better if you do?*" Eyes blazed as he sucked in hard breaths. "*I killed a mortal...I killed a man...*"

The walls around me closed in. This was it...this the truth I was dreading. "Who?"

"What difference does it make?" he snapped.

"I said, *who?*"

"Commissioner Neil Jordain," he said.

I shook my head and stumbled backwards. No. No...*no.* He set me up. He set me up this entire time, and I'd just given myself to him. "Why?"

He didn't understand what he'd done. He didn't care, just opened his mouth and out poured the truth like poison. "When Judas showed me that photo of Evie, I knew something was wrong. She was walking with a basket under her arm. But when I looked closer, that's when I saw it. They'd marked her. They marked my little sister." He lifted his hand, shaky fingers pressed against the corded muscle on his forearm. "There were three dots glowing under her skin. They cut her. They branded her."

Empty words spilled free as I tried to understand. "The Commissioner?"

He nodded. "Those under his control bear that same marking. I'd seen them here, seen them fight. Seen them fall to their knees when they knew there was no way out. If they had to choose between him and death...they all chose death."

It was the same mark as the man spying on the Ancient, and the same one as the dead man in Chuck's closet.

"So, I went to visit the Commissioner," Bond's words invaded. "I shoved the photo in his face and the bastard just laughed. Can you believe that? A mortal laughing in *my* fucking face. He told me to come inside, said he had something I needed to see. He led me to his study like I was a dog on a leash. Then he pulled out another photo and handed it to me." Bond turned and stared at me with glistening eyes. "And I can't get the image of that photo out of my mind."

There was part of me that didn't want to know. "What was it?"

"They'd drugged her." He winced. "They tied her up and shoved needles in her veins like all the other girls they eventually turned into drug mules or prostitutes. She didn't look like my sister anymore, but a stranger who'd lost their way. So I killed him. Ripped out his fucking throat, all because of an image of a girl who once was my sister... but is now a stranger to me. Now, they feed her drugs because they know hurting her would keep me in line."

I shook my head. I didn't understand. "But what does that have to do with me? Why me?"

He stilled, confusion cut across his gaze. "What do you mean, why you?"

"*Do you hate me, is that it?* Do you blame me somehow?"

"Blame you?" He was lost. So utterly lost.

"You set me up. You doctored the CCTV footage. *You* put me at that house and at that crime scene. I didn't want to believe it was you. I came here hoping it wasn't. I came here...I came because..."

Agony filled his gaze. "No," he whispered. "No, not you too."

"They had me in that police station for hours. My entire life on display. Slayer came for me, *do you understand what that means? Slayer...came...for...me!*"

Pink skin turned ashen with the name. He shoved out a hand, slamming it against the lockers as his knees gave way.

"I wanted to believe it wasn't you," my bitter words slipped free. "I would've given anything for it be someone else. But it wasn't, was it?"

"I didn't know," he whispered. "I swear to you on all that I have left in this word, I didn't know you were set up."

"How can I trust you? How can I, if it's so damn easy for you to walk away? You say you didn't have a hand in all this, then prove it. Stand with me now. Help me figure out who the Hell is behind it."

I waited for him to crumble. I waited for him to break.

But he straightened his spine, and looked me in the eye. "It's all my fault you were dragged into this. And it'll be my responsibility to get you out. But my sister..."

I stepped forward, hope blooming like a poisoned flower

inside. "We get your sister free, and then we come for those who did this, and we bring them down."

We were two lonely immortals against a tsunami of terror. How would we survive?

Bond stepped forward, reached out and grasped my hand. "I wish like Hell I hadn't dragged you into this chaos."

"It wasn't you who did. But we're the ones who need to get out of it now. We're the ones who need to fight."

His gaze slipped past me. "I know where to start."

He dropped my hold, and I reached down to step into my sneakers. I knew exactly who he was talking about. The same thug and his goons who threatened me earlier.

He shoved the locker closed and then stepped forward. I grabbed my pack from the floor, slipped it over my shoulders and followed close behind. A Bear and two Wolves. They had no idea what was coming for them.

We'd tear this castle apart brick by brick if we had to.

And we'd start right here.

I followed him through the swing door and then along the alley. The crowd screamed and roared, throwing fistfuls of money into the air as yet two more immortals suffered in the name of sport.

Footsteps thundered on the steel stairs as Bond climbed. No one cared about him now. No one paid him any mind. He was forgotten, just as they all were forgotten the moment they were carried from the ring.

Bond reached for the door handle, pushed it open and I followed him inside.

Gold filled my view. Gold carpet, gold walls. The place made me feel sick stepping inside. Gold, gold, gold...thick rings on the Bear's fingers, and the chains around his throat.

His two goons stood beside him as he reclined in his

leather seat, his smug expression making a nerve dance on my temple.

"Come to grovel and ask forgiveness?" the piece of shit snarled as I closed the door behind us.

"Not exactly," Bond answered carefully. "Tonight was the last fight you'll ever get from me. I've hurt for you. I've maimed for you, but from this moment on I'll kill for me. I'm prepared to leave this place untouched, you can have your blood sport. You can have your hounds. I want what I'm owed. I want my sister."

The Bear's jaw clenched, and the muscles in his neck tensed. He pushed forward in his seat, arms placed on the desk. "Get the fuck out of my office. I'm not in the mood for jokes." He glanced over to his goons who gave a grunting chuckle.

The sound of their sniggers were like claws raked down my spine, and that nerve at my temple twitched and jumped, pushing me closer to the edge.

"Isra," Bond called and stepped forward, drawing the massive Bear's gaze. "I'm not leaving until I have her."

The goon with a trimmed Mohawk stepped forward. "Is that a threat?"

"Take it any way you want," Bond murmured without shifting his gaze from the Bear. "Take it rolled up into a tight little ball and shoved up your ass for all I care."

There were no sniggers now, no laughter. No smiles. Only a savage snarl from the Wolf. I kept my eyes lowered, head down, pretended to reach for Bond's arm in a display of defeat.

They paid me no mind, just like I knew they would. Because all they saw in me was a pathetic female Vampire. The Wolf stepped forward, coming so close I could reach out and touch him.

"One more word, *Beta,*" he snarled. "And I'll tear your fucking throat out."

I stared at the carpet now to keep my rage invisible. The gold fucking carpet that glistened and shone.

"What the fuck is wrong with your girlfriend?" Isra snarled. "The bitch looks like she's quaking with fear. You quaking, little one?"

He shoved up from the seat and steeped around the desk. Goosebumps danced across my skin under his gaze. "You're a pretty thing, if you got rid of the rags and beaten down look."

He reached for me, thick massive fingers trapping my jaw in a cruel grip.

A warning growl slipped from Bond. In the edge of my view his eyes were wide, watching me. But he knew what they didn't...and they made a terrible mistake.

"Kill him," Isra commanded. "But the bitch is mine."

I opened myself up, to the rage and the power. I opened myself to the flicker of Hekate inside me, and this time she didn't let me down.

The Wolf lunged for Bond as the floor under my feet trembled. I slowly lifted my gaze to the warm brown eyes of the Bear.

There was a tremor there, a flicker of...*fear* as Bond let out a savage roar and lunged.

The walls and windows shook. The second Wolf grabbed my arm. I turned into him, letting him touch me with all he had, and then I drove my fist through his chest.

Power rippled through the air like a shimmering mirage. Isra's hand fell as he stumbled backwards. But the Wolf was all mine. Ribs shattered, his heart a pulsing tremble on my hand. One sickening yank and the muscle ripped free and the beast was falling, wide-eyed and pale, his knees buckled and he crashed to the floor. Blood spurted from the open hole I left behind, spraying all over the golden carpet.

"You made a mistake," I murmured and lifted my hand, the heart still pulsing, sucking nothing but air. "You hurt someone I love."

Brutal, sickening smacks on flesh filled the room as the two Wolves crashed into the desk, spilling pens and glass tumblers everywhere. But once the Night Witch was summoned there was no pulling her back.

"You still want me?" I growled, but the voice wasn't mine. "You still want *this bitch?*" I opened my hands, the heart now silent as it hit the floor. "All the women...all the girls."

Isra stumbled backwards, smacking into the towering leather seat as a *crunch* of bone echoed behind me. I didn't turn, didn't look at Bond. All I saw was *him*. He glanced to Bond and then back to me. Now he knew the real monster in the room. *Now* he saw me.

He took a step forward, clenched his fist and then charged.

I stepped fast, moving light, and lunged into the air. Fangs punched out as I reared my head upwards and then struck, like a Viper in a pit.

Blood rushed to fill my mouth, but this time I tore the flesh on the side of his neck free. He thrashed and wailed, charging to slam me into the wall of trophies and glass. I closed my eyes as the sting of pain slashed along my arm.

But there was no stopping Hekate, even if I could. I leaned closer. "I summon thee, squirming, slashing, Vipers and Cobras. I summon thee, Anaconda."

Out of the corners of the room they came.

The Bear under my grasp cried out, stumbled and

stepped on a writhing serpent. It reared upwards, spliced eyes blazing with hate.

Over and over they struck, until I released my hold on the power and his neck. They weren't really there, only a figment of his imagination, but the grip on my chin as he stared into my soul worked both ways.

He looked into my eyes and saw an endless abyss...and I looked into his and saw everything.

Every woman he used.

Ever girl he abused.

Every lie.

And every secret.

But most of all I saw his weaknesses.

As the Bear fell to the golden carpet, shuddering, shaking, death smiled at him.

Bond gasped for breath. The Wolf still at his feet. My lover looked at me, and then reached out a hand.

CHAPTER FOURTEEN

MOON CALLING

THERE WAS A LIST...A LIST OF NAMES.

Wildberries, the word sat at the top and Bond couldn't speak; Evie's name was third on the list.

Labored breaths fought against the silence. A moan came from behind me. I looked over my shoulder to Bond, to what was left of the office, to the two Wolves knocked out, and felt that rage settle deep inside me once more.

Isra lay motionless, his chest no longer rising. There was only the fall for him now. Only the endless night and whatever Hell waited for him. With that thought running through my mind, I felt nothing but peace.

I turned away from the torn skin and broken body, wincing at the pain through my chest. Blood coated my hands and ran down my fingers. But it wasn't mine.

He lifted his head and looked at me, his eyes flooded with despair and desperation. The paper shook in his hands. "They have her here."

I placed my hand over his to steady him, then stared at the address. "I don't recognize the location," I admitted.

"It's a compound on the fringes of the city." He folded

the paper and stuffed it into his back pocket before reaching down on the desk and picking up several others. I scanned the page. *Saffron*. A different address and more names underneath.

"Fuck, how many locations are there?" I murmured, hatred curling through me. These assholes just took who they wanted... With no care of those they abducted or their families. They saw them as replaceable, objects for their own gain.

Bond's gaze swept over the torn up room, the blood, the bodies. He held no remorse, and I didn't blame him. I trembled with anger; they'd deserved so much worse.

"We need to go." Bond took my hand and led me out of the room. We rushed down the steps while the crowds cheered around the ring, the grunt of the fighters, their agony.

It wouldn't be long before the guards discovered Isra dead and notified the council. So we needed to get to the compound fast.

We slipped outside into the night where the moon shone like a star, so damn large that the craters were visible tonight. It was beautiful.

Bond dragged me alongside him, our steps thumping into water puddles in the back alley, splashing our jeans. It reeked of garbage, but it overpowered the Bear's blood caught in my nose.

Bond grabbed his keys and a flicker of lights winked in the shadows, revealing a black sedan. We moved fast, and I pulled open the passenger's seat then jumped in. Bond dove in behind the wheel, and he shoved the key into the ignition. The engine roared to life.

Strapped in, he swung the car onto the road and we took off. I glanced back, the alley was swallowed by darkness and there was no sign of anyone following. No alarms had gone off yet... But it wouldn't be long.

Bond's bruised knuckles turned white as he gripped the steering wheel, racing, swerving around slow cars.

Not long now.

I reached over and set my palm on his thigh so he remembered he wasn't alone. Not anymore. None of us were.

The city lights blurred as we rushed past. Soon, we left behind the traffic and storefronts. Houses and open fields accompanied us.

"How far is it?"

"Fifteen minutes," he murmured, his attention never leaving the road.

The occasional car zoomed past in the opposite direction, the van shuddering as a truck raged past.

Tension was a balloon in the car. And I knew... I knew right now he was running as fast as he could to get his sister. We were so damn close I could touch it, but nothing was guaranteed.

When Bond finally eased off the gas and swung a hard left, I perked up in my seat, ready. He killed the lights and we drove slowly along a gravel road, the car bouncing beneath us, the suspension creaking. Oversized warehouses flanked the road like giants crouched in the shadows. Trees filled the void between the buildings.

Bond pulled up and parked beneath a low hanging tree and killed the engine. "We walk from here."

I pushed the door open and closed it slowly behind me to avoid making a sound. When I stared out into the distance, I found a large compound that looked like an oversized box. Floodlights lit up the enclosed yard, revealing all corners, chasing away shadows. Razor wire.

Guards with machine guns stood watch inside the perimeter.

"Shit, how do we get past them," I mumbled.

Bond slipped his hood over his head and placed a finger to his mouth. Fear coiled tight in my gut that we wouldn't find a way in.

We moved. Fast. Stealthily, we kept to the shadows and traveled in a line, Bond taking the lead.

Not a sound could be heard; the night sat deadly silent like it knew what we were doing. A black shadow flew overhead...a bat, then another. But we kept covering the distance. We'd find Evie today and rescue her. We had to.

If I had a heart, it'd be slamming into my ribcage right now, pounding the hell out of my chest.

An ocean of trees backed onto the compound, curling around the sides.

Bond glanced back and pointed to them. I nodded and we were off again, fast steps. One after the other, I darted across the open ground smothered by the night.

The air felt brittle, as if it could snap, and fear sank in my chest waiting to take over. Not fear of being caught, but that we'd come this far and it was too late or... we failed.

Bond ducked behind an oversized tree and I pressed up against him, his hands on my shoulders, his breath on my neck.

"We need to get closer."

I looked out from our hiding spot, my gaze jerking back and forth over the grounds, taking in the guards... the glowing eyes—immortals, four of them with huge hellish machine guns, the building was closed up, windows drowning in darkness. Three stories to the compound, and four armed guards out front.

I pulled back. Bond was pumping his shoulders up and

down, rolling his head in a circle. The bruises and cuts on his face darkened under the shadows, his hands clenched.

"We can't take them on with sheer force," I whispered. "We'd fall before we reached the wire fence."

He glanced back. "Stay here. I'm going to check the surroundings for another way."

"Be careful."

He zipped over to the next tree and then another before night swallowed him.

I crouched low and looked back at the building, at the dark windows. No guards would be inside. They'd need lights on to keep watch, so that meant the watchmen were just outside. They two stood near the door, chatting, while the other two walked the property line, looking out into the night for any movement.

An ambush wouldn't work. Maybe a distraction? Disabling them of their weapons was the trick.

The air grew still and perspiration rolled down my spine. I sat back on my heels and waited for Bond. Time passed and my gut hurt with each passing second that he'd been gone.

A light crunch of a twig came from behind me, and I spun around, jumping to my feet, fists raised.

"Bond! Shit." I hadn't heard him approaching. "What'd you find," I whispered, but his deflated expression had my stomach locking up with dread.

"No other entry points. Windows are only on the top floor. Only one way in." He stared toward the building, and I swallowed hard.

"I somehow doubt they do guard changeovers in the middle of the night."

He nodded and stared at me, not saying a word, and I wracked my brain for something... anything.

"Power," he murmured. "You used it earlier. Can you draw on it now?"

I thought back to the battles, the power coursing through me, and the witches... "Oh, hell yeah." I tapped my pockets, remembering when I visited them last, I was given a pack with some survival items, along with a Moon glass.

"What is it?" Bond murmured.

At the bottom of my pocket, I fingered the plastic zip lock bag folded around something hard and pulled it out.

"Found it." I showed Bond the little pack. "Moon glass. No idea what it is, but the witches said it would help provide a boost."

I pulled it open and drew out the glass when a sharpness bit across the meaty side of my index finger from its sharp edge. "Ouch."

The atmosphere suddenly shifted around us, charging with a powerful energy that ripped at my flesh. I exchanged a confused look with Bond.

He was trembling and staggered backward against a tree, his eyes rolling back into his head.

I reached out a hand for him and grabbed his arm.

Electricity zapped between us, throwing us apart. We stumbled, my body riddled with power, swelling, rocking me like I might explode.

"W-what's h-happening?" The air was electric, so thick it smothered me.

It raced down my body, my legs, my arms and tore through the woods around me. I swallowed the scream pushing forward. My knees gave out while the moon pulsed overhead. New energies approached, racing toward us.

Energy traveled through the air and snapped out in every direction in a sudden sonic boom.

Bond crumbled to the ground, groaning.

It shook the trees into a frenzy, startling the birds out of the trees.

It bent and warped and flattened the wire fence around the compound.

Guards were on the floor, writhing.

A brightness came from overhead where the moon seemed to ripple.

"What the fuck was that?" Bond pushed himself to his feet and stared at the sliver of glass in my hand. The bead of blood slid down to the meaty part of my palm.

"I don't know."

Bond's eyes grew wide as he stared up into the sky. The moon grew brighter, turning into a spotlight in the heavens, and it let out a thunderous boom. I flinched at the sound.

Stars faded with the glare, and my skin rippled.

"Did you see that? Did you feel what I did?" Bond's voice quivered. Not much scared my Wolf, but this left him unsettled.

I saw it... felt it and looked down at my hand holding the Moon glass. The blood trickled along my palm and up my index finger, seeming to slide back into the tiny nick on my flesh. The wound closed up, knitting back together before my eyes.

An instant later, there was no cut, and my skin was smooth again like it never happened at all.

What the hell?

Bond was at my side, both of us glancing out toward the compound where the four guards scanned the surrounding woods.

"You were looking for something to draw power from," he murmured.

"I have no idea how I did that." I accepted his outstretched hand and climbed to my feet.

"Let's use it to get inside."

I nodded when a distant wolf's howl carried across the night, through the woods. Bond lifted his chin, sniffing the air, listening to the haunting tune.

He turned back to the building. "New plan. Use your power to make the guards come into the woods, one at a time and I'll be waiting down by the shrubs and take them down."

Stillness wrapped around me, the currents of energy still skating over my skin. I'd never felt such energy before.

"Mor! We do this now." Bond's frantic words pulled me back to him.

Studying the Moon glass, I curled my fingers over it, the sharp edges cutting into flesh. With the draw of blood came that rush of a new power. The blow of energy cracked within me, shredding me. It pulsed on my fingertips and felt like fire raced through my veins.

This was magic.

This was me.

I sensed the world around me like the faintest touch.

Bond darted from my side, weaving his way through the shadows toward the shrubs near the compound.

Digging deep within me, I found the energy that felt like liquid. I jerked my head up toward the compound and stared at a huge son of a bitch, carrying a massive gun, sweeping the grounds. Two of the men raced around to the back of the building, while the third man scanned the opposite end of the yard.

I shut my eyes and called him to me, the threads of energy curling around him like vines. It pulsed under my skin, and I felt his muscles, his arms and back, as if I touched him myself.

I opened my eyes, and the guy was stumbling forward like a drunk, swaying and tripping over himself.

Bond looked back at me from his hiding spot in confusion. I'd never done this before, but at least he was moving forward.

The gun slipped from his grip and fell to the ground, but he kept moving, trampling over the bent fence. The barbed wire caught on the hem of his pants, and he kept moving, letting it rip. I drew him closer like an invisible lasso held him. My whole body trembled, and with each use of energy, I felt my muscles weakening, my power fading. The moment he reached the shrub, Bond leaped out and jumped on him, both of them falling into the bushes, vanishing.

"Hey!" the second guard yelled and raced toward them. He had a radio in his hand. Shit, he was calling for backup.

Fuck! I dug deep once again and refocused on the second guard, but two others raced to the front and approached their friend. They talked to him, then shoved him as he stood there unresponsive, still gripped in my power.

The tallest of the crew pulled out a handgun and shot him straight in the head.

Ripped from my connection, I stumbled, and a sharp pain slammed into the side of my head.

I dropped down, crying with pain, grasping my head, rocking back and forth, swearing a bullet had lodged into my brain. But it couldn't be, right? I pulled my hand away, expecting blood, but my palm was clean.

It was just in my mind.

All in my mind.

But it felt so real.

Crawling back up, I stumbled and pushed the hair out

of my face. Okay, that was a new experience. Looking across to the compound, the guards were shoving Bond across the yard, a machine gun aimed at his back.

I shuddered, my eyes tearing, and agony shredded my insides. I ran toward them, fear colliding in to me. This couldn't be happening. It couldn't.

Bond fell to his knees, a gun pointed to the back of his head.

Tears blurred my vision as power skipped over my arms in response. I jutted them out, hurling everything and anything I had at the guards. An explosion of energy struck them like daggers, piercing their chests, their heads.

Terror clung to me, driving me forward, and I screamed in fear that I'd lose Bond.

Lines of electricity, the color of the sun, coiled around them, throwing them off their feet. It was too late for them. They were convulsing on the ground, gagging and frothing.

They fell silent fast, laying there unmoving. And I staggered, the power dissolving around me.

I should have felt remorse, except, without a doubt, they would have killed Bond, so I felt nothing. I ran into Bond's arms, sending us both reeling backward, but he held me tight.

"I thought..." Tears rolled down my cheek, my insides burning up. "I thought I'd lost you." My tears just fell.

He cupped my face with both hands and wiped my tears with his thumbs. "You saved me. I knew you would." He kissed my head, my nose, and lips.

I ached already, and our fight had only just begun.

Bond took my hand and we rushed to the front door. He kicked it in without ceremony. A gaping black mouth greeted us, and we ran inside, vanishing into its embrace. We had to finish this. Tonight.

Bond's thundering steps led us toward a set of stairs, and I took them two at a time. I gripped the handrail, pushing past my missed steps.

He took my elbow and held me close as we navigated through the dark. He sniffed the air and we turned left on the second floor.

Rushing blindly, I followed Bond. We burst into a room but it took me several moments to make out what I looked at.

Single beds with flaking metal frames lined the wall. Figures lay under the bedsheets.

They made no sounds and lay in silence, but something didn't feel right. It raked over my flesh like nails.

"Evie," Bond called out and raced straight ahead, knowing exactly where she slouched. The middle bed right below the window.

I kept looking over my shoulder, expecting someone to burst in after us. My skin crawled, but we weren't going anywhere without Evie.

Her head jutted up, and she sat up so fast, the sheet fell to her waist. Chains bound her wrists, keeping her imprisoned, but her eyes... they glowed under the moonlight pouring in through the window.

She stared Bond with savagery, her lip curling upward, and she growled at him like she *was* a beast. There was no humanity left in those eyes.

CHAPTER FIFTEEN

UNDERGROUND

"What have they done to her?" Bond whispered and stared at the girl in the dark.

Glazed eyes looked back at us. Evie curled her lips and snarled. "Stay away from me. Stay the fuck away."

He stepped closer, hand reaching out carefully. "It's me, Evie. It's Bond."

"Bond?" The growl ended, and the frightened voice of a child slipped free. She pushed upwards until the chains around her wrists snapped taught.

"Oh, baby," he whimpered and stumbled closer.

But the second he moved, the beast returned. She gnashed her teeth in the air, and yanked on her bindings. This time there was no desperation to get to him, and no need to be saved.

Bond stilled barely an arm's length from her body.

"Bond, maybe we should..."

"No," he answered. "We take her. I don't care if I have to knock her out and carry her feet first."

She punched out when he neared her.

"Easy." He grasped her wrist, and then eased his hold.

"I'm not going to hurt you. I'm here to save you, take you back home. You remember home, right? Back to the woods...back to the pack."

"The pack?" she whispered and stared into nothing.

He moved slow, pulling the bed sheets from her body and then moaned at the bruises along her legs. In the dark they looked black. Blotches and black veins marred her beautiful skin.

"You're gonna be okay." Bond's voice broke. "I'm going to take care of you."

He grasped the chain bolted to the wall and with one massive heave he yanked.

But the steel didn't give, holding strong. He tried again, giving it all he had. I hurried forward, grasping where I could.

"Ready?" he murmured.

I nodded, tensed my thighs and yanked. The bolts gave way with a *snap* and both Bond and I stumbled backwards. Evie thrashed her arm, broken chain lashing the air like a damn weapon.

"Don't touch me!" she screamed at the top of her voice. "Don't you touch me! Don't you hurt me!"

The sounds were deafening in the quiet night. Bond lunged, slamming his hand over her mouth. "Quiet, Evie," he snarled against her ear. "We're trying to save you for fuck's sake."

Still there was no calming her. Muffled roars hummed against his hand. I hurried around the bed, grasping the other chain and glancing over my shoulder.

"Gotta hurry," Bond urged, desperation glistened in his gaze. "They'll be here any moment."

Gotta hurry... It took two of us to break one side, but this one was just me. I wrapped my hands around the thick links and ground my stance. Power hummed through my body, and I let it ripple out into the air.

Evie stopped thrashing, stopped screaming. Her eyes went wide, and she turned her head to stare at me as I inhaled hard and then pulled with all I had.

Metal links snapped taught. I pulled and pulled.

"Come on, Mor. You can do this."

Muscles screamed along my back. I saw stars in my eyes. My hands were burning, clutched around the steel, still I never gave up, pulling until *something had to give.* And with a tiny shudder of power through my chest *something snapped.*

I stumbled backwards, dragging Evie's arm with me. Bond moved fast, sliding one hand under her knees and the other around her back. He carried her, lifting her from that filthy mattress and carried her from Hell.

I hurried from that room and out into the hallway as the sound of heavy footsteps echoed through the dark. Bond moved fast and quiet, lifting Evie's body until she was pressed against his chest.

Soft, soothing words slipped free, reassuring her he was never leaving, not ever again.

He'd keep her safe, he murmured. He's always keep her safe.

We hurried through the doorway as a roar came from behind us. *"Hey! Stop right there!"*

There was no stopping as Bond raced through the doorway and along another hall, passing room after room. Girls cried out, they snarled and whimpered. Some begged.

The sound of all those voices whirled around inside my head. They were beaten, starved, most were drugged while I laughed and joked and fought a pride of Lions, oblivious to what was going on in my city.

I punched my sneakers against the floor, and it was *my City*. I was the Understudy. I was the one responsible for the Vampires, and I didn't need to search every room to know my kind were here. I could sense them, just as I could sense the power of the moon above me.

Just as I could sense Bond.

"This way." He sucked in hard breaths and then sprinted through a doorway, only this one led to a set of stairs. He gripped his sister who was starting to fight him, kicking her legs, slamming the broken shackles against his shoulders and his back.

Gunshots rang out, smacking the wall beside my head as I raced through. All I could see was Bond hurt and bleeding, running with gunshots in the back. I stepped left and slowed until he was a step ahead. *Boom!* One more shot tore splinters of wood from the door frame as I passed.

I ducked, fighting the desperation to cower from the shots. I'd not let them hurt him, not anymore. Evie kicked and bucked, tearing one leg from Bond's hold as he stumbled sideways down the stairs.

She fought him, wrestled and screamed, and behind me, the Wolves with guns charged.

"*We don't have time for this!*" Bond roared.

He clenched his fist, holding her as she wailed. The ratchet of a shotgun behind me punched fear into my mouth. I spun, turning on the Wolf as he raised the muzzle high and tool aim.

"*No!*" My scream shuddered the walls, sending debris raining down. As I took aim, and then charged.

Footsteps thundered inside my head. I drove my fist through the air as I lunged, hitting the Wolf in the chest.

Hot metal slammed against me, and we were falling, hitting the ground with a *thud*. And even though I knew different all I could see was Isra's face. They'd hurt Bond. They'd bitten him, tortured him.

I lashed out, striking his face and his head. I punched him until Bond's screams broke through. "Mor! *Enough!*"

I stilled then, seeing the blood and terror on the Wolf's face under me. I shoved backwards, revulsion filling me, and turned to see the man I loved.

"It's okay," Bond murmured. "He's dead."

I shoved upwards, and then slipped in the trail of blood.

The stench was all around me, in my mouth, along my throat...in my veins.

They tried to turn Bond into a cold blooded, killing machine.

They wanted him to be just like them.

But he wasn't like that.

I was.

I stumbled from the sight and then turned as Bond dragged his sister down the stairs once more. She stared at me with terrified eyes, whimpering in the back of her throat as I stepped near.

"Stop it." Bond shook her as he stumbled from the lower floor and out into the courtyard.

Gunfire opened up, muzzle flashes blazing in the night. I stumbled, swinging my gaze as three massive Wolves leaped in their beast form and charged. Paws pounded the ground.

The moon pulsed above me, growing brighter the more I felt its call.

Bond dropped Evie to the ground, his gaze staring at the three beasts heading this way. There was no way he could take them...not on his own.

A blur of midnight cut through the courtyard. Sickening snarls and gnashes of white fangs shined, as a massive

Alpha collided with the biggest of the Wolves and they fell to the ground.

Another Wolf charged after the first, tearing through the open gate of the compound. Black fur mingled with white, I knew who it was in an instant...*Nero...*I wrenched my gaze to the towering black beast...*and that's Judas.*

Bond shifted in an instant, punching brown coarse fur through soft pink skin. The snap of bones echoed as he dropped to all fours and raced toward them, shifting into his beast as he met the last Wolf.

Gunshots rang out across the other side of the compound. I lifted my hands, panic tearing through me and the moon shimmered and shook in the sky. I felt that connection now, like nothing I'd never felt before.

Bright sparks of gunfire blazed as I drove all my desperation and energy through the air. The night shimmered like a pale barrier around my three Wolves.

I flinched with the sting as bullets hit my power, but they didn't pass through, until with a crash the power was gone.

And so were the Wolf guards.

Three of them lay still on the ground as Judas shook thick, midnight fur and then turned his head. Silver shone over brown eyes, finding me before he turned back.

Nero gave a chuff and padded toward me. I stumbled forward, hand raised, prepared to do whatever I had to.

Blue eyes blazed in the night. Nero towered next to me, pressing a cold, wet nose against my arm, and nuzzling my hand.

"I'm okay," I whispered, watching as more guards raced from the darkness. "But we need to get out of here, we need to move."

He gave a *ruff* and turned away. Bond was already running,

shifting as he lunged toward me. I was seized by the image of the beast turning into the man. Ears pulled back, skull flattened. He shoved upwards as his body morphed upright. He knelt and snatched what was left of torn jeans from the ground.

Two seconds and he stepped in each leg, yanking them higher, leaving his chest bare and grasped his sister once more.

"No, stop it. You don't understand!" She wailed and kicked as he lifted her from her feet and threw her over his shoulder.

A howl ripped through the night, savage and tormented. I lifted my gaze to Judas as he stood between the swarm of guards filling the other side of the compound and us.

"Judas," Bond called, waiting for a second before he carried Evie toward an open door in the hallway.

Nero gently nudged my arm with his snout, driving me forwards, leaving Judas behind. As gunshots rang out once more, Judas turned from the carnage and followed.

I hurried, racing after Bond as he tore through a darkened doorway and slipped away into the dark. Terror found me as I raced after him. Footsteps thudding as I found his outline and turned into a maze of hallways.

We raced through tight spaces, the wolves fur scraping the walls as they pushed through and in an instant the floor titled down. Bond snarled, heavy footsteps thundering as we raced lower and lower.

The passageway grew wider the lower we dipped, cold packed earth was on either side as we hit the ground at a bunker.

"Through here." Bond scanned the darkness finding another passage spearing off straight ahead. But Evie was done being carried.

"Let me down, Bond. *I said, let me the Hell down!*" She slipped from his grasp in the center of the room.

"You're not going back there." Bond glared at her and snarled. "What the Hell has gotten into you?"

"You don't know," she snapped and reached up to scratch the inside of her arm. "I'm sick. I'm sick and they take care of me."

I followed her outline as she moved toward the entrance of the hallway and looked over her shoulder. Footsteps thundered behind us as someone shouted. *"They're underneath!"*

I caught the word *"Explosives."* Before I turned to Bond. "We have to get out of here...Bond...we have to leave."

Evie lunged through the dark hallway. Panicked steps frantic as she slipped away. Bond raced after her, and I followed, hunted by the two Wolves at my back.

Shouts rained from above. But Bond was all I saw as I scurried after him, plunged into the darkness.

Seconds felt like hours. I passed a small darkened doorway on the left as we pushed through, fighting to get to her.

Boom! The floor shook. The walls trembled.

Bond's wide eyes were all I saw as he turned, grasped my shoulders and drove us through the next doorway and into a room.

The Wolves lunged, clawing the dirt as the second detonation tore through the air.

Boom!

Dirt rained down as outside this room, the ceiling came crashing down. I sucked in dust, choked air as Judas and Nero turned. The doorway was not an opening anymore.

Massive boulders crammed it. There was no way we were getting out of here, not anytime soon.

The ceiling rumbled, ground shaking. I stumbled backwards, bumping into Bond. His arms went around me. My two Wolves backed up, snarling, fangs bared at where the doorway had once been. I waited for the ceiling to fall, for us to be buried in here, and the seconds slipped by.

The Wolves' snarls ended.

Heavy gasping breaths followed, we waited for what seemed like an eternity until Judas turned and pierced me with the glint of his silver eyes.

We stood like that, facing each other, the words we'd failed to say in our gaze.

"I'm sorry," I whispered and saw the twinge of rejection. "I had nowhere else to go."

"Judas, you don't..." Bond started until a savage sound rumbled in his Alpha's chest and spilled free.

"Don't blame him," I whispered. "If you want someone to blame, then blame the people who've done this. Blame those we're trying to find. They set me up, made everyone believe I was a murderer, made me think I had to walk away from everyone close to me. Made me think I had to be alone."

Nero shifted first, shaking thick, coarse fur as he did, and stood in front of me bare. "He doesn't blame you," he answered. "He blames himself."

A stab of agony coursed through me. I turned to the Wolf I loved and lifted my hand. "No, none of this was on you."

He stepped forward, hulking shoulders rolling as he moved. His breath blasted my face as he held my gaze. Was this over? Had I ruined everything between us?

Until with a slow movement he lowered his head and

pressed his massive skull into the center of my chest. I was frozen, feeling the life in him ripple through, it wasn't just an act of submissive, it was an act of love.

My hand rose, fingers sinking into his thick pelt. I ran them over his head and down his pointed ears as tears welled in my eyes.

"I never want to feel like that ever again." My husky words burned as they tore free.

I wrapped my arms around his neck and shoved my face against him. I held onto him as I shuddered and shook. I held him as the thudding of his heart changed. I held onto him as hard muscles and smooth skin replaced inky fur, and the Wolf slipped from me, leaving the man behind.

Judas lifted his hand, and tilted my chin, soft warm lips brushed mine. "Never again," he hummed the words. "You hear me, Morwenna Livingstone, or the next time you don't put your trust in me will be our last."

I flinched with the brutal sting of his tone.

He meant it.

I knew he meant it.

There would be no more Judas, no more Wolves. Our pack would be broken and it was all because I hadn't learned to trust. "No more," I whispered against his mouth.

The kiss deepened, hungry, and desperate. I needed more...so much more.

Even though this cavern could break and crumble any moment I gave in to him. Fingers gripped hard muscle. He bent, hands sliding under my body. "I can smell my beta all over you. Here..." He ran his hands down my hair, and then slipped to glide along my breasts to cup between my legs. "And here."

I shuddered under his touch as Nero pressed against my side. I leaned my head backwards. "He needed me."

"And now, so do we," Nero whispered.

Hands worked my shirt, pushing the fabric higher, another at my waist, buttons popped, zipper was pushed lower. Bond was there, with his scent of hunger and pain. I turned my head, kissing him.

Judas bent his head, pushing aside my bra to take my nipple. A shudder coursed through my body. I sank to the ground, falling. Hands held me, breaths warm on the back of my neck. Judas pushed my jeans low, and then bent, sliding my sneakers free.

"You're ours, Morwenna," he growled. "And it's about time you realized that."

He moved between me, and I was more than ready. Nero gripped my breasts, kneading as Judas slid between my thighs. There was no waiting, no touching, just animal lust as he drove his body inside.

"Say it," he growled and thrust harder. "Say you belong to us."

"I..."

Nero bowed his head, warm tongue lapping at my peak as he took me into his mouth.

"I belong to you."

"Now you know it," the Alpha growled. "I'll take my fill."

Hips thrust upwards with savage blows, and the sound of smacking filled the air. Bond moved in, kissing me, touching me, until I lost the feel of my body, until there was nothing but them and the desperation of being together again.

CHAPTER SIXTEEN

BEST SIGHT IN THE WORLD

"Don't ever let me go," I murmured, my back pressed against Judas' chest, and he held me tight.

"We're in this together. Thick or thin. Right or wrong. We share everything from now on." Warm lips pressed against my head. For a second I closed my eyes and pretended we weren't down here in the dark and the cold.

Rasping breaths filled the room. Everything was cast in shadows and darkness.

Bond sat next to me, knees pulled toward his chest, his expression darkening, while Nero kicked rubble across the floor.

"Someone will come," Judas murmured.

"When?" Nero barked. "We've been down here for hours."

Silence answered.

The longer we waited the more tired I grew. I'd forgotten sleep, forgotten the comforting embrace of nothingness. My eyelids grew heavy. Judas' embrace was so warm and nice.

"What's that?" Nero barked, wrenching me awake.

Judas shifted, sliding out from behind me to stand, I followed, and all four of us moved to the wall covering the entrance.

Another thump from somewhere outside the room, the ground under our feet quivering.

"What is that?" Bond asked, scanning the ceiling as dust rained down on us.

I stepped closer and set my hand on part of the collapsed ceiling and when the next boom came, the stone shuddered under my touch.

"Someone's trying to get through." I glanced over my shoulder to the Wolves. "We need to help them."

"And if it's the guards?" Nero asked, grabbing his phone off the ground, the light throwing shadows around us.

"Then we fight," Judas instructed, and I agreed. Staying hidden here left us vulnerable and cornered.

When the thud from outside came again, rocks, large and small, unlodged from the top and tumbled toward us.

Bond looped his arms around my waist and swung me away, his feet moving fast.

The clank of rock colliding into rock echoed around us, and small plumes of dust burst into the air.

I coughed as Bond set my feet on solid ground and we all backed away, deeper into the room.

A murmured voice came from outside the room.

"Did you hear that?" I asked, and the Wolves nodded, our attention glued to the entrance.

A tremendous boom slammed into the stones again, shaking the entire room, and more rocks unlodged from the top, slamming to the ground, bursting into bits and sending shards in every direction.

Another explosion, and another broken part of the wall dislodged, falling away, and in its place a ray of light shot outward through the small gap in the stones blocking our entrance.

I bounced on my toes.

"Mor!" Ava's voice came through the gap in the rocks blocking the doorway.

"Oh my god, Ava!" I scrambled forward, joy slamming in my chest, hearing her voice was like an angel's whisper. Dramatic, but fuck, damn I'd missed my friend. "All four of us are down here," I called out.

"Stand as far away as possible. Chuck is going to try to make this hole bigger so you can all crawl through."

"Okay." I stepped back.

Nero grabbed my hand and drew me to the rear of the room.

I met my Wolves' gazes, all of us huddled together. "Ava and Chuck are gonna tear down that whole damn building," I muttered, unable to stop smiling. Yeah, I still had shit to sort out, but I wasn't alone now, and I let myself have this moment, to remember what I fought so hard for.

The thumping started again, over and over, and each time, the hole widened. Rocks fell away.

Another thump, and a stones crumbled to the ground. The room trembled around us, and more dust cascaded down onto our heads and shoulders.

"Okay," Ava called out. "You need to get out fast. It's looking unstable." Her panicked voice had us all scrambling forward.

Bond's hands fell to my waist and he raised me to sit over his shoulders. "Hold onto the wall and we'll push you up."

My palms flat to the cold concrete, the Wolves grasping my legs and ass, pushing up. Easily reaching the gap, I grasped it with dear life as my body wobbled and pressed myself forward, wriggling through the hole.

I glanced down at Ava on the other side of the barricade, who smirked so wide it was contagious. "Hey gorgeous," she muttered. "Looks like you need a hand."

Chuck stood there, sweaty and dirty, a thick metal rod by his feet, the weapon he'd used to dislodge the rocks. Jagged walls and broken stones lay around them.

"Heck yeah." I pushed myself through the hole, slithering forward. Chuck lunged up and grabbed my arms. He pulled me free, and I started falling down. He swooped me into his arms and lowered me to my feet with ease.

Ava slammed into me, her arms locked around my shoulders, squeezing the life out of me. "Never ever do that again. You scared the shit out of me by vanishing like that."

"I'll try." I broke from her and found Bond pushing through the hole. Chuck grabbed his arms and yanked him out.

Bond stumbled down but managed to catch his balance.

Ava gasped and spun to turn her back to Bond, who stood there naked.

Nero was next. "Just take it easy, I gotta protect the family jewels." He smirked, and Chuck chuckled as he reached up. When he yanked him out, Nero lost balance and rolled down before hitting the ground like a sack of potatoes.

I rushed over and helped him up. He just dusted himself off. "Thanks, babe." He winked before swinging around to help Judas through.

A loud crack boomed around us, and the ceiling trembled. My world tilted, and I darted toward the wall where Judas wriggled through. The hole offered a tight fit for him. He had one arm through and he pushed himself forward.

Nero rushed toward him with Bond and together they seized their Alpha's arm, then hauled.

The walls quivered, dust raining down on us, and I froze on the spot.

Chuck ran forward like a god, brandishing the rod, and propelled himself higher.

Ava whimpered next to me, clutching my arm.

Chuck slammed the end of the weapon into the jammed rocks inches from Judas' side.

They shifted, a loud groan erupting.

And everything crumbled.

I screamed and rushed forward just as Bond heaved Judas free. The guys all fell and landed in a heap on the ground, groaned and rolled, hitting a wall.

"It's gonna come down," I cried out.

The guys were scrambling to their feet, and we all ran for our lives, darting toward the stairs.

A blast boomed behind us, and I glanced back as the ceiling came down fast, taking everything with it. A pillar of dust exploded, concealing the mess. That disaster came too close to taking Judas. Too damn close.

We slowed down on the next floor, most huffing for air. Bond charged upstairs, arms pumping by his side, determination in his rushed stride.

"Bond," I called out.

"Evie," was all he said, scaling the steps like a mountain climber.

"She's already safe," Ava yelled after him.

Bond halted and turned, his eyes narrowing. "Where is she?"

"At the local hospital," Chuck answered. "Along with the other women chained up in the building. We got them to safety before we found you in the basement."

Bond's shoulders eased as he hurried back to our sides, his breathing no longer speeding. "I'm going to see her."

"I'm coming too," I added, and everyone else nodded in agreement. Without a word, we moved out in a mass. This was what I'd missed. Us as a unit, tackling everything together.

***

A HEAVY DOSE of antiseptic and sickly sweet cleaning detergent filled my nostrils. Bond entered room 307, and we filed in after him. Four girls shared the room, all asleep. We turned to Evie who was hooked up to an IV line. Her muscles twitched under her skin, her eyes moving left and right beneath her lids. Bond sat on the bed next to his sister and took her hand in his. His head hung low, and he didn't say a word.

A nurse wandered into the room, startled at seeing us crammed in. "I can get you some spare chairs," she suggested, her gaze shifting between my Wolves and Chuck.

I shook my head. "It's okay."

Bond twisted around to face her. "How long before she can come home?"

"As soon as the doctor ensures he's found the right level of treatment for her. Are you family?"

He nodded. "Her brother."

"Okay good, I have some forms for you to fill out." She pivoted and left the room, but the door swung open once more.

Someone tall, powerful, and wearing a grimace entered.

"Dad?" I blurted. "What are you doing here?"

"Morwenna, you need to come with me." Darkness coated his voice, and I trembled. He was my dad, a Master Vampire, and when he was scared, the whole city trembled.

"What's going on? You're scaring me." I stepped closer, accepting his hand, his cold fingers curling around mine.

"We've been summoned before the Supernatural council."

My insides felt like barbed wire, and Ava was at my side, pressing close.

"We've been called to stand trial for murder and conspiracy to commit murder."

CHAPTER SEVENTEEN

SUMMONING

Dad's silence was a blade to my throat.

He stood near the window in his study, staring outside, deep in thought and hadn't spoken for the past fifteen minutes.

I paced to the door and back, fear strangling me. All the recent events spiraled in my mind, but I'd missed something. A thread that connected them all. "Someone's framing us, framing *me*."

"Shh." He turned around, shadows heavy under his eyes. The warning on his face said it all.

We couldn't talk openly, not here, not anywhere. There were ears in every location. I understood, but it didn't help when we were about to stand trial for something we didn't do.

"What's going to happen?" Dread clung to my insides. I hated feeling this weak and vulnerable.

He walked closer and drew me into his arms, holding me like he used to when I was younger. When I felt as if nothing in the world could touch me. But his grip was a little too tight, like he was trying to capture the memory of how I felt against him, nad he was worried he'd lose me.

His fear raced up my arms.

"Everything happens for a reason." His somber voice softened, and his hands fell away from my back.

I glanced up at him, studying how he controlled his expression with such perfection, anyone else would see him as a Vampire with power. But I saw someone different. A father who grasped onto anything to save his daughter, trying to keep his head above water. I saw the pain in those eyes and the love he had for me.

"Please, Dad, I need to know what to do. We need to beat them. I'm stronger now."

His brow furrowed, and he turned away from me again, staring out into the garden. "You don't understand what it feels like to be torn apart, never knowing if your next step will be your last."

I closed the distance between us and reached for his arm. He was strong and powerful, but I sensed the light tremble in his body. His position was sought after... the rising new Vamps would kill to claim the title of Master, while the established families played games to take over his dominion. Always the struggle for power, the new versus the old. It'd been this way for as long as I knew. But this was different.

"Help me understand," I muttered.

"Then pay attention. There's a reason you gained the position of Understudy," he continued, his gaze finding mine as he turned. Unspoken words stirred behind his eyes, and I couldn't decipher what he wanted to tell me. I curled my hands. *Think. Think. Think.*

Vlad had insisted I wasn't the right person for the role,

and while his harshness shredded me, what exactly did the Ancient want if I wasn't good enough?

A soft knock sounded at the door.

"Come in," Dad called out.

Helena strode inside, carrying a silver tray with a teapot and two cups. She set them down on the table and looked at me. "Your mother insisted I bring you a cup of blood tea." Without hesitation, she poured the syrupy liquid into each cup, the metallic tang heavy in the air, then set them on coasters on Dad's desk. With the pot back on the tray, she carried it out and shut the door behind her.

"Drink your tea while it's warm," he insisted. I collected a cup, gulping down the minty blood tea in one go.

Dad handed me a tissue, and I wiped my mouth before tossing it into the trash.

"What am I supposed to do at the trial?" My mind swam with images of the prosecutor throwing so much fake evidence at me that something might stick. I'd never been to a Supernatural hearing, and I had no idea what to expect.

"When we get there, you're to say nothing, you understand? Nothing. Let me do all the talking. You let me take the fall."

I stiffened my back, stilling. *Let me take the fall.*

"No, you can't," my frantic response rushed out.

He grasped my arms, his eyes drowning behind pain. "Just listen to me. You do as I say, sweetheart."

My throat thickened at hearing the agony in his voice and my gaze never wavered from Dad.

"I'm trusting you'll figure this all out. I know you will. You're smart and brave and fierce, just like your mother. But there's a time for battle, and a time to plan. This is that time, Morwenna. This is our time to be meek and mild, and not show what we're truly capable of. I know you can do that. I know you can. Believe me when I tell you I love you, and I never meant for any of this to touch you the way it has."

"What do you mean? Please, talk to me properly. I'm not a child anymore. Help me understand."

Dad smiled at me, his lips strained sadly, and his arms hung limp by his side. He leaned closer and kissed me on the cheek. "Hurry now, go get ready. Our escort will be here any moment."

I wanted to be strong for him, say something that might brighten the moment, give him confidence, yet I couldn't even convince myself of those things.

He turned back around and went to stand by the window, looking out.

My words never came, but the tears fell. I wiped them and left the room, dragging myself to my bedroom.

"What's wrong with me?" Why couldn't I just figure it out. What was I missing? I'd written a list in my mind of everything, gone over it dozens of times, yet it wasn't enough. The carousel of dread circling my thoughts didn't help either.

With an overexaggerated sigh, I pushed myself to the walk-in wardrobe and stripped.

Get ready, Dad said. So, I'd dress the part... what exactly did one wear to a trial that could get me wrongfully accused of murder?

I grabbed my black suit pants and stepped into them, pulling them up my legs. The police Commissioner never believed me, and everyone back at the press conference where I addressed the mortals thought I was a child. They didn't take me seriously, but they would now. I reached for a simple white button-up shirt.

As I pushed my arms through the long sleeves, I kept

going through the clues, Dad's words, and still I missed the link. How was it all connected?

The more I pushed, the less it made sense, but my head was messed up. And those damn tears refused to stop falling. I buttoned my shirt with hands so shaky I couldn't get the buttons through the hole.

"Get it together," I mumbled under my breath and wiped my eyes before trying again. Pushing, I got one button in, and then the next and all were done in seconds. I was a Livingstone and I didn't crumble in the face of adversity. I fought.

Holding my head high, I ran fingers under my eyes. "No more tears either."

From the hanger, I pulled a black fitted jacket and slipped it on, before grabbing my black Gucci heels. I stepped into them and strolled up to the mirror.

I looked strong and ready to take on anything. A true Livingstone.

Taking my brush, I combed the hair off my face and spun it into a bun at the back of my head before securing it with bobby pins. Next, foundation would conceal the puffy bags under my eyes from the tears.

By the time I finished and stepped in front of the full length mirror, I resembled a strong Vampire to be taken seriously. A Supernatural who would never murder someone.

I was a different girl to the one who once lived under this roof. Someone I was proud of no matter what anyone else said.

"Morwenna," Helena howled through the house. "Your guest has arrived."

I grumbled under my breath. Slayer. "He's not my guest," I called out. Shaking myself, I stared in the mirror one last time.

"You got this. You're strong. Beautiful. And everyone will see they made a mistake." I swallowed hard and walked across the bedroom and into the hallway where Chuck waited. He shoved off the wall and smiled down at me.

I'd been used to seeing him in the house growing up, but now it felt different. He wasn't just my guard and Dad's protector, but a friend. Someone who loved my best friend and had become one of us. He reached out and pulled me into a hug. I threw myself at him, his embrace strong. *Don't cry. Don't cry.*

"I have something for you," he mumbled, and I pulled back to see what he was talking about, blinking hard to keep the tears at bay.

In his palm lay a silver hair pin in the shape of a dagger. "The tip is tainted with something deadly should you need it." He reached over and wove the pin through my hair.

"I love it." My voice crackled.

"Morwenna," Helena cried out from downstairs.

Licking my dried lips, I squared my shoulders, and marched downstairs ready to do this. "Guess it's time."

CHAPTER EIGHTEEN

THE COUNCIL

I LIFTED MY GAZE TO THE PALE EYES OF THE henchman as he curled his lips and sneered, "Gotcha."

Dad cleared his throat behind me, drawing the piece of shit's gaze. "We've been summoned by the Council, and we're obeying that summons. I'd prefer it if you didn't speak to my daughter. Any concerns, you may address with me."

I saw it now, that hidden current of tension. Slayer didn't like my father, and I didn't have to turn my head to see the feeling was mutual. I fought the need to reach up and touch the thin, poisoned-tipped blade plunged between the twist of my hair.

I'd not give in. Not behave how they expected me to. With my father's desperate plea running through my head I lowered my gaze and stepped through my front door to the waiting limousine.

Dad followed, leaving Mom behind. I wanted to turn to see her standing in her office window on the second floor above, but that would be weak and cruel.

Movement came from my right as Chuck strode out of the darkness, his expression a mask of cold, barely controlled rage as he met my gaze and then turned away and opened the rear door.

Fear filled me like I'd never felt before. My knees locked. I couldn't move...until Dad gently grasped my elbow and whispered. "Keep walking sweetheart, we're almost there."

My throat tightened, tears threatened to spill free as I stepped onto the vehicle and slid along the plush leather seats. Dad climbed in behind me as Slayer strode toward the door.

But Chuck moved fast, putting his hand across open door and growled. "Sorry, this one's all full."

There was a sneer, and a curl of his lips before Slayer turned on his heel, black leather trench coat flapping with the movement, before he strode away.

Chuck glanced toward me and then gently closed the door.

I should've known Dad wouldn't let us go alone, should've known there was no way in Hell Chuck would allow that to happen. I turned my head, and lifted my gaze to my father's.

But there were no smiles, no laughter, there wasn't even reassurance. This was the man I'd grown up with, the man that others saw. The iron fist of control. The calm before the storm.

And I knew it was raging, lashing his mind with chilling hunger.

I turned my gaze to the front of the car as Chuck climbed in and started the engine. I'd never been to the Council before, I didn't know many who had, but these men and women held my fate in the palm of their hand.

Murder

And Conspiracy to commit murder.

Those were our shackles, that was our fate. I thought I'd be able to figure this out, that I'd find the real man behind the Commissioner and Isra, except I had nothing but a hospital filled with drugged women, an underground fighting pit filled with death, and the glowing three dot tattoos.

I'd failed Bond.

And I'd failed us.

I reached over and clasped my dad's cold fingers, so unlike a Wolves. He opened his hand, and slid his touch away. This wasn't time for emotion. This was the time for planning. This was a time for survival.

I sat back against the seat, swaying as Chuck drove. Minutes turned into hours, still Dad never spoke. He turned his head and stared through the dark tinted windows. He may as well be a thousand miles away.

The car climbed as we wound around a mountain and then down the other side. I lost track of how long we were driving, two, three hours until the car started to slow.

"Remember," Dad murmured, making me flinch. "You say nothing. Let me to do all the talking. No matter what."

"No matter what," I repeated as the crunch of gravel echoed under the tires and the limousine braked to a stop.

The driver's side door opened, the sound setting my nerves on fire. Footsteps came alongside of the car until our door opened silently.

Dad shifted his body and slid out, standing for a second to button his jacket. "You know what to do," he murmured, never once turning his head.

There was no answer from my bodyguard. My heart sent out a *thud* as I craned my head to see his face, but he was out of view. Dad stepped forward and turned, and held out a hand for me.

This felt like the end, for the both of us.

I had nothing to plead with, nothing that I could ever hope to do in exchange for my father's life. My body felt like lead, weighed down with the truth. For me it was over. For me there was no denying what they saw.

I had no proof to tell them otherwise.

I grasped Dad's hand and slipped from the car. Flames licked the sky from open pits along the driveway. The place was ominous and broody, and a faint orange hue danced and glistened against midnight windows.

Headlights splashed us from behind and then passed as Slayer drove his car around the side of the building and disappeared.

Gotcha, the word filled me. I couldn't shake the smug expression on his face, or the excitement in his eyes. He hated me. He truly hated me...and I had no idea why.

Chuck pushed the car door closed behind me. Dad stepped forward, still gripping my hand. *Oh, so now he wanted to comfort me?* But the touch wasn't tender, it was controlling as he steered me forward and up the wide steps to the expansive building in front of us.

The place didn't look ancient. Just old. Dark brown brick caught the firelight shimmering as we moved. There was a walkway in the belly of the building, and pebbles crunched under our feet as we headed for the dark.

Chuck moved in behind us, half a step away and at my side. My stomach was hard, breaths short and shallow. I'd close my eyes and pray for a miracle, if I could. I'd faced death before...Hell, I'd faced Lions before. But *this* was different, this was an enemy I couldn't see.

Dad climbed the stairs, taking me with him, and as he strode toward two gigantic double doors at the end of the path, they opened for us. There was no hitch to his step, long, sure strides carried us forward as we stepped into a building and then headed along the foyer toward the end of the building.

The doors closed with a *bang*. I jumped at the sound and tightened my grip on Dad's hand. He kept walking, never slowing, never jumpy—powerful, stoic, and cold.

I turned my focus to two more doors as they opened at the end of the hall. The soft hue of more flames flickered inside.

Dad and I stepped into a darkened room. My heart clenched at the rows of statues in the gallery to my left, and then the towering bench on the far wall at my right...in the middle was a single box, with a small swing door open and waiting.

The shadow shifted at my left as we entered and the flames around the edge of the room grew brighter. The haunted face of the Ancient came toward me. I flinched, a scream trapped in the back of my throat. Dark unfathomable eyes shone in the light. He stared at me, and then lifted his gaze.

Something passed between him and my father, something in the glint of a stare, something I didn't understand.

"This is the Supernatural Council," boomed a voice from the raised podium at my right. "And we will have order."

The room seemed to shimmer and shake. A wall of guards appeared around us, ice white eyes glinting in the dark as they watched us. Goosebumps raced along my arms as the room brightened, revealing faces I didn't know.

They watched us from the galley, unflinching and uncaring, they picked me apart inside their mind. One guard stepped forward from the other side of the room and strode across the divide, stopping at the open gate of the box.

My legs trembled, thighs ached. Dad stepped forward, but I couldn't move. Frozen with fear, I trembled where I stood and tried to not fall apart.

"Dante," the voice from the podium commanded. "Is something wrong?"

Something wrong? Something wrong...no, not at all your Highness. Just our fucking lives hanging in the balance...

"No, Justice," Dad answered. "We are simply taking a breath."

"Then take a breath in the box," he commanded. "And let this all be done."

I couldn't feel my body, couldn't feel my feet moving, but somehow they were, somehow I followed Dad to that dais in the middle of the room with its waiting door open, like a greedy mouth and stepped inside.

The moment the gate snapped closed, the air seemed to shift. From the darkness of my right, someone stepped forward. Black eyes, pale skin, and pale lips curled into a sneer. My heart lunged, smashing against the inside of my chest as Thorin dipped his head in greeting.

What the fuck.

Green eyes glinted with savagery beside him. Brylee stepped forward, and the same sickening grin twisted her ugly face. "No," the word slipped from my lips.

Dad's hand clenched around mine as a voice boomed. "*Quiet!*"

They were all here, Thorin, Brylee...Slayer standing behind them, half in the shadows.

I jerked my gaze to Dad, desperation roaring through my body.

"You understand the charges?" The Judge barked down at us.

I shook my head, this wasn't right. *This wasn't right.*

"Yes," Dad answered. "We do."

"And you're fully aware of the consequences for these actions?"

Dad was silent.

Cold.

Empty.

Black eyes glinted with life but there was nothing there.

"Are you aware of the consequences of these actions?" The Judge leaned forward, smooth skin revealed in the orange light. The glow caressed his face, revealing him to me.

My stomach plunged. Smooth pale skin and eyes that shone with life, he was no older than I was. A hundred, two if that. So young...so much power.

"Dante," the tired voice of the Ancient whispered behind us. "I beg of you, don't do this. Don't give in. You are all that stands in their way."

"Morwenna Livingstone," the Judge snarled. "You are hereby stripped of your title of Understudy."

"You can't do that," the Ancient shuffled his frail body forward. "*I decide the titles. I decide the laws.*"

"You are a tired old man." There was glee in his tone as the Judge leaned further. "You are weak, your powers are weak...*your hold is weak.* It is time for a new beginning. *A change.*"

I knew what that glint was in his eyes now.

It was mania.

It was power.

It was greed.

"And you are you hereby relieved of your duties, Vlad," the young Judge murmured. "Slayer."

The whole world seemed to spin as the henchman moved. The grind of sharpened steel filled the room as a wall of warriors moved in to protect the Ancient.

"Not yet, as they say," Vlad muttered.

"Out with the old, old man," the Judge snarled. "And let's welcome in the new."

Guards lunged and gunshots rang out. The glint of steel on steel sent sparks through the room as Slayer and his men attacked. I flinched, spun, watching the Ancient's warriors swarm around him in defense.

"No!" Dad roared beside me, but his gaze was locked on the young Vampire sitting high up on his throne. "Judge, this is not the way. This is not how we do this."

"It's how *I* do this," the sickening Vampire answered, long fangs slipped over blood colored lips. "You will make your choice, Dante. You will succumb to my demands and *pick a fucking side!*"

That cliffhanger!! Oh, we bet you can't wait get your hands on the next book... the conclusion to the Beautiful Beasts Academy. And you won't be disappointed. We have lots of excitement coming your way. Danger, sexy times, and answers...

But we'll let you in on a secret... we have something else planned. Something after book 6 in this series... So keep an eye out.

Don't forget to join us in the Kila Foung Facebook group, we're posting extra scenes in there that you won't be able to find anywhere else.

See you there!

Kim and Mila, a.k.a Kila Foung

One man stands between the barbaric rule of Supernatural Council and the weakening line of the Ancients—my father, Dante Livingstone.

The time for peace is over. Swords have been drawn, and we stand at the edge of war.

I've fought Demons. I've battled lies. I survived with those I love standing beside me. But this time it's not enough. This time I'm up against a force not even Hekate can help me win.

I'm falling on my knees, desperate to find a way out of the dark. I don't want to believe it's over…I can't…not until the very end.

Read the gripping conclusion of the Beautiful Beasts Series today!